Dear Reader,

There was a time when I thought nothing was
more beautiful than the Chesapeake Bay on a
warm summer afternoon, or the green stretches
of the Maryland countryside—places where a
man could think, make some decisions. But
that was before I laid eyes on Liza Callahan—
for the second time. The first time was when
she was no more than fourteen, a gangly,
gawky girl. But now, Liza was all woman, but
certainly not all mine. And unless we can get
this love thing worked out, I'll be back on the
bay, thinking...alone.

Thatcher Hamilton

Maryland

1. ALABAMA
Full House • Jackie Weger
2. ALASKA
Borrowed Dreams • Debbie Macomber
3. ARIZONA
Call It Destiny • Jayne Ann Krentz
4. ARKANSAS
Another Kind of Love • Mary Lynn Baxter
5. CALIFORNIA
Deceptions • Annette Broadrick
6. COLORADO
Stormwalker • Dallas Schulze
7. CONNECTICUT
Straight from the Heart • Barbara Delinsky
8. DELAWARE
Author's Choice • Elizabeth August
9. FLORIDA
Dream Come True • Ann Major
10. GEORGIA
Way of the Willow • Linda Shaw
11. HAWAII
Tangled Lies • Anne Stuart
12. IDAHO
Rogue's Valley • Kathleen Creighton
13. ILLINOIS
Love by Proxy • Diana Palmer
14. INDIANA
Possibles • Lass Small
15. IOWA
Kiss Yesterday Goodbye • Leigh Michaels
16. KANSAS
A Time To Keep • Curtiss Ann Matlock
17. KENTUCKY
One Pale, Fawn Glove • Linda Shaw
18. LOUISIANA
Bayou Midnight • Emilie Richards
19. MAINE
Rocky Road • Anne Stuart
20. MARYLAND
The Love Thing • Dixie Browning
21. MASSACHUSETTS
Pros and Cons • Bethany Campbell
22. MICHIGAN
To Tame a Wolf • Anne McAllister
23. MINNESOTA
Winter Lady • Janet Joyce
24. MISSISSIPPI
After the Storm • Rebecca Flanders
25. MISSOURI
Choices • Annette Broadrick

26. MONTANA
Part of the Bargain • Linda Lael Miller
27. NEBRASKA
Secrets of Tyrone • Regan Forest
28. NEVADA
Nobody's Baby • Barbara Bretton
29. NEW HAMPSHIRE
Natural Attraction • Marisa Carroll
30. NEW JERSEY
Moments Harsh, Moments Gentle • Joan Hohl
31. NEW MEXICO
Within Reach • Marilyn Pappano
32. NEW YORK
In Good Faith • Judith McWilliams
33. NORTH CAROLINA
The Security Man • Dixie Browning
34. NORTH DAKOTA
A Class Act • Kathleen Eagle
35. OHIO
Too Near the Fire • Lindsay McKenna
36. OKLAHOMA
A Time and a Season • Curtiss Ann Matlock
37. OREGON
Uneasy Alliance • Jayne Ann Krentz
38. PENNSYLVANIA
The Wrong Man • Ann Major
39. RHODE ISLAND
The Bargain • Patricia Coughlin
40. SOUTH CAROLINA
The Last Frontier • Rebecca Flanders
41. SOUTH DAKOTA
For Old Times' Sake • Kathleen Eagle
42. TENNESSEE
To Love a Dreamer • Ruth Langan
43. TEXAS
For the Love of Mike • Candace Schuler
44. UTAH
To Tame the Hunter • Stephanie James
45. VERMONT
Finders Keepers • Carla Neggers
46. VIRGINIA
The Devlin Dare • Cathy Gillen Thacker
47. WASHINGTON
The Waiting Game • Jayne Ann Krentz
48. WEST VIRGINIA
All in the Family • Heather Graham Pozzessere
49. WISCONSIN
Starstruck • Anne McAllister
50. WYOMING
Special Touches • Sharon Brondos

MEN
MADE IN AMERICA

DIXIE BROWNING
The Love Thing

Maryland

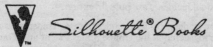

Silhouette® Books

Published by Silhouette Books New York
America's Publisher of Contemporary Romance

SILHOUETTE BOOKS
300 East 42nd St., New York, N.Y. 10017

THE LOVE THING

Copyright © 1984 by Dixie Browning

ISBN: 0-373-45170-9

Published Silhouette Books 1984, 1993

All the characters in this book have no existence outside the imagination of the author and have no relation whatsoever to anyone bearing the same name or names. They are not even distantly inspired by any individual known or unknown to the author, and all incidents are pure invention.

® and ™ are trademarks used under license. Trademarks recorded with ® are registered in the United States Patent and Trademark Office, the Canadian Trade Marks Office and in other countries.

Printed in the U.S.A.

Chapter One

Tossing a suitcase into the back seat of her elderly car, Liza was torn between a slightly hysterical desire to laugh and an even more pressing need to weep. Several old platitudes concerning ill winds and silver linings came to mind as she backed recklessly out into the side street that the apartment she shared with Carol Davenport faced. More in an effort to calm her nerves than anything else, she began a muttered listing of things she should have done before taking off.

Leave a note for Carol that she'd gone sailing with Todd after all and would be back by Tuesday. Done. Water plants. Done. Close bathroom window. Done. Refill birdfeeder—oops! Forgot that one. Turn refrigerator down to save energy, since both of them would be out all weekend. A penny saved and all that, and now that she'd been fired again, through absolutely no fault of her own, every penny was doubly important.

And she'd liked the job! Considering that selling and occasionally even modeling high fashion clothes in the newest branch of Barnes and Taylor was about as far from designing houses as anyone could get, it had been a good job. And after all these years, she'd all but kissed her lifelong ambition to study architecture good-bye.

Oh, well . . . back to the classified ads . . . or the employment agency. Not both, though. She'd learned from frustrating experience what it was like to apply at an agency for any job connected with building or designing houses and then snatch at a waitressing job from the classifieds when nothing was forthcoming, only to have the agency call and ask if she was free to go to work immediately with a construction company involved in urban renewal.

With one last, half-rueful recollection of the embarrassing scene an hour or so earlier, in which she had tried to explain her reason for being extremely late three mornings in a row, she relegated the lost job to the past. Casting off her impotent anger and stamping out any hint of panic, she regarded her future with carefully contrived optimism. At least she'd have a holiday before putting her short, slightly freckled nose to the grindstone once more. And she wouldn't allow the few doubts she'd had about her relationship with Todd to surface now. This was no time for negativism!

Todd Hardely, one of *the* Hardelys of Virginia—FFV, U.Va., UDC, DAR, and all that, according to the social pages of the *Pilot*—had sauntered out of the gilded and muraled elevator and onto the plush carpets of the second floor of Barnes and Taylor one afternoon three weeks ago to announce that he wanted something in a cranberry red, preferably chiffon, and as to size...his eyes had skimmed the bemused faces of the small sales staff and lighted on Liza Calahan. "You, love...you model them for me, will you? Right coloring, right size, right *everything,*" he had stressed with a slow smile of discovery.

That had been the start of a whirlwind courtship that had left Liza limp and palpitating. Oh, not that she hadn't been rushed before. After all, she was twenty, not bad looking, and had been on her own since she graduated from high school—since before that, actually, although that was a private arrangement between her and her stepmother.

Todd, as if recognizing that she might feel slightly out of place in the rarefied atmosphere of his own social set, had taken her on picnics, on a walking tour of every marina in the Greater Norfolk area, and to small, out-of-the-way night clubs where they danced in each other's arms until the early hours of the morning.

Small wonder she'd been late Wednesday morning. It would have taken dynamite to wake her up. She'd fallen into bed exhausted at three after an extended and frustrating session of saying no in Todd's Porsche. Still, she had said it and made it stick. Being thrown on her own at such an early age had made her doubly aware of the pitfalls that awaited an unwary girl, and even though she was almost a hundred percent certain she loved Todd—and he declared that he was crazy about her—she had to take things slowly, cautiously. She had no one to fall back on, no one to turn to for advice or sympathy if things went wrong. Besides, all her life she'd been cursed with a hopelessly impulsive nature, and in matters of this sort she made a conscious effort to use the small store of common sense allotted her.

"So what are you doing high-tailing it up to Annapolis after a man you'd never even heard of a month ago?" she muttered against the dyspeptic sound made by her faded pea green sedan. It had been the car that had done her out of the high prestige, low salaried position with Barnes and Taylor, which, while not what she wanted permanently, had had some lovely fringe benefits. The car had stopped dead on Thursday, halfway to the new mall where she worked, and she'd had to wait while Rudy from the garage came and hauled it away. He'd called later to say something about a pinhole in a water hose that sprayed a fine mist on her distributor cap, all of which meant nothing to her.

"How much and when?" she'd asked the cheerful mechanic whose station was on the corner of the block where she lived.

"Cost of the hose and the tow truck. I'll throw in the labor. Leave her until middle of the morning, and I'll check her over for you. You ought to trade her in, Liza. Thing's got over a hundred thousand on her."

That meant taking a bus to work, and because she was frantic she'd be late again, she'd impulsively jumped aboard the first bus that came by and ended up miles away from Cloverleaf Mall. Despite the best intentions in the world, somehow something always managed to go wrong for her!

It was late in the afternoon by the time she reached Annapolis. Traffic was at its peak. Liza, her nerves abraded by the tension of the long drive, the morning's upsetting scene—one *never* got used to being fired—plus a growing realization of what she'd committed herself to, took a deep breath, then expelled it shakily. She began to look for signs that would lead to a yacht basin.

It hadn't occurred to her to get more explicit instructions to where Todd was berthing his sloop, the

Hardely Ever. When first he'd invited her to spend
the holiday weekend sailing with him on the Chesapeake, she'd had to refuse. The store was busier than
it had been since opening day, getting ready for the
Columbus Day sale and fashion show in which Liza
would be modeling sportswear. She found fashion
shows a dead bore, but they paid extra, and if Mrs.
Kellog found her five-feet-eight, one hundred and
eighteen pounds a suitable rack on which to hang
overpriced designer togs, who was Liza to complain?

With the sudden loss of her job, though, came the
realization that fashion wasn't all *that* boring. It was
infinitely preferable, for instance, to starving. It was
probably sheer bravado that had made her throw a
few things into her car and take off after Todd. He'd
been nasty when she'd refused to go with him, and
they hadn't parted on the best of terms. This would
be a chance to mend things between them. He'd
hinted that the trip might be a milestone in their relationship. Did that mean he'd planned to propose to
her? He had said they might be seeing his brother
and sister-in-law, and that was significant . . . wasn't
it?

Oh, darn! She'd been following a trail of pictorial
signs that promised to lead her to a yacht basin of
some sort, and now she'd missed it. How was she
supposed to get to the waterfront, anyway? The

whole blasted skyline bristled with polished aluminum masts, and all she could do was corkscrew around narrow, colonial streets between narrow, colonial-style houses.

Water, water everywhere, she fumed. And then, eureka! The last sign had pointed in this direction, and there at the end of the street were high wire fences with a gate house. Beyond was an assortment of boats. She hesitated momentarily and then decided that even though there was no yacht club sign on the gate, this had to be the place.

The guard stopped her. "Naval Academy property, ma'am. Civilians not allowed beyond this point."

With a fresh set of instructions and a growling stomach—she hadn't taken time to eat since her hasty, insufficient breakfast—Liza counted off the turns and twists in her head until she came to a more impressive gate, this one, too, complete with guard.

"Hi! I've had a devil of a time trying to find this place! D'you happen to know if Todd Hardely's sloop is here? He was supposed to have left Portsmouth yesterday." Her agitation increasing, Liza found she had to convince the skeptical gatekeeper that she was neither a groupie looking for a swinging yachtsman nor a subversive intent on toppling the so-called upper classes.

"Who could believe this?" she muttered angrily to herself as the man turned to his cubicle for the third time to call on the house phone, this time to check with the harbormaster about whether or not Mr. Hardely had already sailed and, if so, for where.

He had. Liza listened with growing dismay as the guard told her that Mr. Hardely had sailed that morning, leaving word that he'd be staying at either St. Michaels or Oxford for the next few days. It was small comfort that at least the man was polite now that he had determined her bona fide connection with a legitimate member of the club.

Liza stubbornly remained on hallowed ground long enough to study her map. It wasn't too far to the Bay Bridge, and once she reached the Eastern Shore, it wasn't so very far to St. Michaels. At least it didn't look all that far on the map. Drawing in a deep, steadying breath that did little to allay the hollow feeling inside her, she took dead aim for highway 50-301 and the bridges.

Somewhere between the Severn River Bridge and the longer Bay Bridge, she felt behind her for the bag in which she'd put an apple and a sandwich. It must have fallen to the floor. With the way her luck was running, she'd better pull over and set the parking brakes before she ended up decorating the hood of one of those tractor trailers that had just about blown her off the highway.

The sandwich was cheese on dark pumpernickel, slightly stale now and not very inspiring. The supermarket's brand of mild cheddar was as far as she dared go toward indulging her taste for exotic and expensive cheeses. The crisp apple, however, made it more acceptable.

She'd eaten half the sandwich and all of the apple when she realized she was no longer alone. A low whine alerted her to the presence of a pathetic animal of ambiguous breed whose starving condition was emphasized by her blatant pregnancy. "Oh golly, honey," Liza crooned through the opened window, "somebody had better start boiling water for you... fast!" Without thinking, she handed out the remaining half sandwich. The dog practically inhaled it from her fingers and then pled silently with large amber eyes.

"All I've got left is an apple core, and I know you don't want that." She tossed the darkened core out the window and groaned as the hungry animal swallowed it whole. Without stopping to think, she reached across, opened the passenger door, and patted the seat. The dog stared at her dumbly until Liza opened her own door and got out, and then it flinched and sidled away, looking back over a skeletal shoulder. Liza knelt and called softly, extending a hand reassuringly until the wretched creature decided she could be trusted. It took another five minutes to convince the poor animal that her best chances for survival lay in allowing herself to be settled onto the front seat of the strange vehicle.

Not until they were headed south on highway 50 toward Easton and St. Michaels on the Eastern Shore did it occur to Liza that Todd might not welcome a flea-bitten mongrel in imminent danger of exploding aboard his thirty-eight-foot sloop. She knew he liked dogs; he'd told her about his Brittany spaniels, proudly listing the Grand National and Field Trial champions in their bloodlines.

"Your pedigree might leave a little to be desired, darling, but nobody could turn you out at a time like this." There was no collar, nor any sign that the poor bitch had worn one in the past. Still, she was docile enough.

"We've got a lot in common, Mrs. Mutt. Neither of us has much in the way of prospects at the moment, but take it from me, just when a gal least expects it, something comes along and she's off and running again. I've hit bottom so many times I'm permanently bruised, but before I know it, I'm scrambling right back to the top again. And if we're lucky, lady—*that's* what I'll call you—Lucky Lady. Okay, Lady, if we're lucky, I'll be sipping tea and munching cucumber sandwiches with Mr. and Mrs. Courtland Hardely the Third and brother Todd, while you bore a pack of overbred Brittanys with the details of your confinement.''

The dog gazed dolefully at her from a pair of trusting amber eyes set in a wrinkled and none too clean coat of wiry brindle.

After only two false turns in Easton, Liza was put on the road to St. Michaels by an accommodating service station attendant. She tried to comfort herself with the fact that at least she wasn't driving into a setting sun. With her pitted windshield, that would have been lethal. The last bit of daylight was rapidly disappearing, and there was a definite feel of Halloween in the pale, newly mowed fields and the bare branches that rose here and there above glowing hardwoods. There was an occasional glimpse of water, reminding her that in the midst of all this lush farmland, she was never very far from the Chesapeake Bay.

Lady grew gradually more confident. By the time they came to the outskirts of the early seventeenth-century community on the Miles River, she'd forgotten her earlier fears so far as to lay a trusting muzzle on Liza's thigh. If the white corduroy wraparound skirt was being smudged in the process, then that was just too bad. Being a dog person himself, Todd would understand. Besides, he'd soon forget white corduroy when he saw the ivory crystalline nylon and lace nightgown she'd shot her month's salary on. And, she admitted for the first time, he would probably see it. No point denying that she'd known all along, from the time Todd had first invited her, how such a weekend would inevitably end. It had undoubtedly been in the back of her mind when, after being fired, she'd taken the elevator to the first-floor lingerie department before word could get out and used her employee's discount one last time. She'd regret her reckless actions later, when she got the bill, but what was done was done.

It was too dark to see very much. There was an impressive gray stone church and a row of attractive-looking shops in what must have been centuries-old houses, but no indication at all of a yacht club or marina. She'd simply have to inquire.

Pulling over into a small parking lot beside the church, she waited until a couple strolled past on the sidewalk and then rolled down her window and called after them. Lady showed signs of aggressive protectiveness and Liza had to cut short her questions, but at least she now had a clue. It seemed there were several likely places, one of which was somewhere at the end of Mill Street, a few blocks farther along Talbot.

Minutes later, she found herself backing out of a narrow one-way street between high picket fences and quaint, well-kept houses. There were cars jammed in every which way and, unless she was losing her feeble mind, a steel band was playing not far away. Its exotic rhythms on the crisp autumn air blended strangely with sounds of laughter, jovial conversation, and intermittent announcements from a loudspeaker that a table for Halen or Larson was ready.

"Lady, have we wandered into the twilight zone?" she muttered, twisting in an effort to back out of the congested dead-end street. "It's not reggae, but it's definitely steel and— All right, all right, I'm doing the best I can!" That was an irate reply to a suggestion from another driver intent on making the same mistake she had made. There was parking space beside the narrow street and she found an empty slot. "Lady, I'll leave a window open for you, and I'll be back just as soon as I check out the boats down there. Be a sweet girl, and I'll try to scrounge us a hush puppy while I'm gone. I definitely smell food around here."

It took less than three minutes to traverse the narrow stretch of asphalt. Liza paused, half in dismay, half in pure fascination, as she surveyed the gay, unlikely scene before her. A rising hunter's moon illuminated dozens of masts beyond what seemed to be a restaurant of some sort. The lower level, a bar where drinks were served and oysters were unloaded from boats, then shucked and served, opened directly out into the street, and it was there that the five-man band played for an enthusiastic throng of people waiting for their tables to be called. They wore foul weather gear, blankets, jeans, and rugged sweaters, and it was obvious that many of them were from the nearby yachts.

At any other time, Liza would have loved it, but by now she was starved and worried and more than a little cold. With the setting of the sun, the superficial warmth had gone, and she was dressed in only her corduroy skirt and a long-sleeved periwinkle blue cotton shirt. Somewhere among her things was a sweater—at least she hoped she'd thought to include it. At this point, she wasn't certain of anything.

The thing was, she had to get close enough to the water to be able to read the names of the assorted yachts she could glimpse through the crowd. Sidling behind a white-haired couple in yellow oilskins who were moving to the beat, she rammed a fast-moving teenage boy and ricocheted off another before making her way safely to the edge of the water. There were half a dozen or so people even there, some feeding the flock of swans and mallards that paddled calmly around the shore and a few taping or taking pictures. By leaning out at a dangerous angle, she managed to read several names, none of which was the *Hardely Ever,* the slightly too cute name of the Hardely's family yacht. She was climbing over a low fence to where the wharf continued around the restaurant when she heard a startlingly familiar laugh behind her.

She stepped on a foot as she hopped back down, muttered an apology, and began to retrace her steps. Todd's voice sounded again, clearly audible in a lull in the music.

"I've had enough of this scene, darling, what about you? Didn't I hear you say something about an early night?"

The answer, and it was unmistakably an answer to Todd's suggestion, came equally clearly in a drawling female voice. "Honey, I've been ready for an early night since five o'clock this evening. Who's hungry, anyhow?"

That laugh again, that achingly, miserably familiar laugh. And then Todd's voice said, "For food, at any rate." The words came from much closer behind her.

Panic sent her pulse racing, and Liza lifted a hand to cover her face. Todd and some woman! Probably the one he'd bought the cranberry chiffon for! She couldn't be found here, she just couldn't! They were only a few yards away, heading her way and she was hemmed in. Reacting instinctively when a large form blocked out her view of the crowd of dancers, Liza lifted her arms and buried her face in the rough surface of an oiled wool sweater. She wasn't even aware that her fingers were gripping solid flesh and bone until a gravelly baritone, sounding more amused than angry, reached her ears.

"If you really want to dance, I think you're supposed to move your feet."

"No," she mumbled, not lifting her face from the warmth of the stranger's chest. In the part of her brain that still functioned, she was aware that this man loomed over her. At the moment, he was a fortress, and the bigger he was, the better she liked it!

A flurry of random notes signaled the end of one number and the beginning of the next, and Liza felt the man's arms close around her. Her tightly shut eyes were starting to burn. She shook her head protestingly. It had been minutes, agonizing minutes. Surely Todd and his girl friend had passed and were safely aboard the sloop by now. With her back to the waterfront, she risked lifting her head.

The man was ready for her. Warm hazel eyes crinkled down at her from an attractively rough-hewn face. "Was it a case of love at first sight, or are you related by birth to an ostrich?"

For a fleeting moment, something nudged at the edges of Liza's stricken mind. Even as she stared up into the stranger's face, she saw a change come over it. If it weren't so absurd, she'd have thought he had seen a ghost, but then, in her present state, *she* could very well be hallucinating.

"Don't I know you?" he asked. She jerked herself from his arms. Things were bad enough without allowing herself to be picked up by some smooth-talking, overaged sail bum.

Muttering an apology, she pulled away and hurtled through the milling crowd, stepping on toes and elbowing her way through rudely in an effort to escape the lighted area before the tears surfaced. She almost ran into one of the drums, righted herself, and stumbled past it. Then, clear of the crowd, she dashed blindly into the side of a van that was backing out of one of the precious few parking places.

She fell awkwardly, not realizing at first what had happened. Several people saw her, and someone banged on the side of the van to stop the driver. Embarrassment came first; then the slow realization of various physical pains overtook the emotional ache that assailed her.

Hands reached down to help her up and sympathetic voices offered conflicting advice until another voice, more authoritative than any of the others, took over and dispersed the small crowd. "Come on now, girl. Sit still until we find out if you're all in one piece." Hands moved over her in a thoroughly familiar manner. In her dazed condition, she was scarcely aware of it. When the stranger knelt and slid an arm under her knees and another one around her shoulders to lift her up from the dirty pavement, she released a shuddering sigh.

"Had your eyes checked lately?" he teased gently as he carried her to a darkly gleaming Mercedes. So far Liza hadn't uttered a sound. For all she knew, she might not be able to speak ever again. Somehow, it seemed easier to allow this good Samaritan to take over. At least he moved with the sureness of a man who knew where he was going and why, which was more than she did.

"I don't think you cracked anything vital, but just to be on the safe side, I'll run you in to Easton General and have the experts give you a once-over."

At that, Liza stirred herself from her apathy. "No. Oh no, I don't think so."

He was pulling out and then they were passing the lot where Liza's car was parked. She protested again, but her voice was incredibly weak. "Save your strength. They might put you through your paces at the hospital. You've just had a shock, at the very least, and unless I miss my guess, you've had more than one. You've got about as much color in your face as skimmed milk."

It was shamefully easy to retreat into the purring comfort of his luxurious car and allow herself to be driven through the darkness. No questions, no explanations. She closed her eyes and felt her mind reject a feeble command to shift out of idle.

Neither of them spoke during the short drive to the nearby town. It was a friendly, comforting silence, and Liza took the coward's way and allowed it to grow. Perhaps he thought she was asleep. Maybe he even thought she was unconscious. Her eyes seemed to want to remain closed and she let them—line of least resistance, laws of gravity, and all that, she rationalized weakly.

A niggling thought surfaced momentarily. Just for a moment when she'd first seen the man, there had been something, some snag in her memory. Hadn't there? Or had it only been his all too familiar line? "Haven't we met somewhere before?" Had he looked shocked when he first saw her face, or had that been her imagination? She could almost have sworn there had been something, some powerful physical jolt, but at the moment she was in no condition to worry about it.

"We're here," he said. "My name, by the way, is Thatcher Hamilton—Thatch, if you're in a hurry." He turned to her expectantly. When she didn't immediately respond, he shrugged his massive shoulders and slid out from under the wheel, coming around to help her out of the car. By now she definitely needed his help. During the short ride, she had stiffened up in more places than she thought possible. Her elbow hurt, her head felt as if it were growing a head of its own, and one of her knees was stinging badly.

"Come on, then. This way." He practically carried her. In spite of a broken heart as well as a battered body, Liza was uncomfortably aware of the powerful spell of his potent masculinity. The blow on her head must have been harder than she thought.

Liza tried to express her gratitude, but she wasn't at all sure her words reached his ears. All too soon, she was taken over by an attractive nurse in a pants suit and whisked away. There was time for no more than a worried glance over her shoulder at the man who had picked her up and brought her here. He was now in a deep discussion of some sort with the admissions officer. He didn't even know her name.

Liza tried to keep up with the efficient nurse and, at the same time, inform her that the man who was admitting her was a perfect stranger. The uniformed woman told her not to worry about a thing. The doctor would be with her in a minute.

I won't worry if you won't, Liza thought with a rise of slightly hysterical humor, but when the time comes to pay the bill, one of us is going to change her tune.

Forty-five minutes later, she hobbled stiffly out to where Thatcher Hamilton waited. Her head had been examined and declared safe, if unsightly, and she sported bandages on both her knee and her elbow.

She had winced, gasped, and swallowed obediently. When he saw her, Thatcher stood and came to meet her, and she allowed him to take her arm. There was something unbelievably comforting about the large, gentle man, and that was a rare enough commodity in Liza's hectic life to be savored while it lasted. If that made her an opportunist, then so be it.

As he held the heavy door open for her to pass through, she brushed against him. The usual hospital odor was quickly replaced by a dash of cool, damp autumn air and the warm, intoxicating scents of a subtle aftershave, tobacco, and good woolens. Liza caught her breath and swayed slightly. Thatcher's arm came around her back as he directed her toward the parking lot. She muttered something about the painkiller she'd been given and hoped the brightly tinted lights disguised the flush of color that burned her face.

"Here we are, Miss Calahan. Watch the edge there." He lifted her stiffly bandaged leg inside without either bending it unduly or scraping it against the door, and Liza watched in drugged bemusement as he came around the hood of the car to take his place beside her.

Chapter Two

At first Liza was too concerned with trying to deal with her own confused feelings to wonder about the use of her name. Thatcher fastened his seatbelt and reached over to do up hers. Then he placed her purse in her lap and switched on the ignition. "Oh, my goodness, I forgot all about it," she mumbled, clutching the small leather shoulder bag.

"Not surprising. By the way, I've got something to take care of the headache, plus all your other assorted ailments, but I suppose you were given enough to hold you for the next few hours." It wasn't a question; it was a statement.

Liza closed her eyes and wondered if she was imagining a note of coolness in his voice. It didn't occur to her to ask where they were going. By this time, she would have followed him anywhere, as long as it was to a place where she could quietly pass out. Not until they were over halfway back to St. Michaels did she remember Lady. "Oh, no!" she groaned. It was the first time she had spoken since they'd left Easton. Not that her silence seemed to bother her companion at all. He was the strong silent type, evidently, which at the moment suited her just fine.

"Something wrong?"

"My dog. I left her in my car. It must have been hours ago!"

"Not all that long, surely. How long had you been there when you...ah, ran into me?" The warm, gravelly voice *was* just a bit less warm and a bit more gravelly than she had remembered.

Liza choked out a small laugh that sounded more like a groan. "Into you and everything else in the neighborhood. Not long...no more than ten minutes."

"I'll take you back to your car, and you can collect your dog and whatever else you need. Then I'll take you home with me."

Her protest was more perfunctory than real. Whatever she'd been given at the hospital to alleviate the pain was making her dizzier by the minute. "I can stay at a motel, Mr. Hamilton."

"With what you have in your billfold, you wouldn't stay long. And what about your dog? I don't know of many motels that welcome pets."

It was all Liza could do to hang onto reality as she listened to the slightly abrasive note in his voice. What on earth was she doing here in the middle of Maryland with a perfect stranger, a lump the size of an eggplant on the side of her head, no job, less than forty dollars in her purse, and a pregnant dog depending on her? Twenty-four hours ago all she'd been concerned about was mending her quarrel with Todd, her ailing car, and her apartment mate's habit of leaving the three rooms looking like the aftermath of a hurricane.

"Well, just for the night then," she agreed reluctantly, "...if you're sure no one will mind. I'll be leaving first thing in the morning."

Thatcher Hamilton remained silent, and somehow it seemed to Liza that the silence was not nearly so friendly. It must be the medicine. The knock on her head—or something—was making her overly imaginative. And there was the bill at the hospital, too. She hadn't any insurance. Her policy with the store had ended with her job, worse luck!

Lady was pathetically glad to see her again. Her sides looked lumpier than ever, and when Liza let her out to walk for a minute before putting her into Thatcher's car, the load seemed to have dropped considerably. She remembered vaguely from early childhood days, when she'd been allowed to have a pet, that that meant labor was imminent.

"Oh, Lord, just what I needed," she muttered to herself as Thatcher came around to collect her suitcase. He'd unlocked his trunk and now, in the lights from his own car, he got a good look at Lady for the first time. If Liza had been in any condition to laugh, she would have howled at the expression on his face. He looked from the dog to Liza and back again.

"Have you lost your mind?" he inquired with stern amazement.

"You don't understand," Liza began, leaning over to beckon the dog and almost falling over in the process. She clutched the side of the car momentarily for support and then called softly. Lady evidently knew her new name, for she came immediately.

Thatcher opened the back door of his impeccable maroon sedan and helped the cumbersome animal inside. Straightening up again, he eyed Liza with a grim expression . . . or perhaps it was just the harsh lights of the parking lot that made his eyes seem so judgmental, she thought hopefully. "Oh, I think I understand well enough—more than you realize. Maybe it's to your credit that you didn't want to leave her at a time like this, but for God's sake, woman, what happened to your common sense?"

It wasn't worth trying to explain, not the way she felt now. It was enough to know that she and Lady both had a place to sleep tonight, and if she had to pay for it by suffering a few derisive comments, then she could take it. Her skin had thickened protectively a long time ago. It had had to. Stepdaughters of selfish, ambitious women learned quickly not to allow themselves to be wounded by cruel remarks. "I don't think I care to discuss it just now," she said as airily as she could. She had behaved like an idiot from the first time she'd laid eyes on the poor man and he had done nothing to deserve it, but she had about reached the end of her rope. She'd apologize and explain tomorrow.

When tomorrow came, however, Liza was in no condition to do either. She had been shown to a bedroom, and at the time she couldn't have said whether it had any other furniture or not. She'd only had eyes for the bed, and it had been all she could do to pull back the spread before tumbling in, clothes and all. There was a dim recollection of someone's slipping off her loafers and unfastening her skirt, and that was the last she knew until she awakened to see a stream of sunlight slanting across a polished pine floor that was partially decked with a pristinely white crocheted rug. The brightness of the light was almost blinding.

Closing her eyes, Liza reviewed the past twenty-four hours. She ached in everything acheable, mental as well as physical. She fought against a cowardly desire to sink back into merciful oblivion and made herself sit up and throw back the covers, noticing for the first time the silky, pale blue sheets and the white wool blanket and spread. The next thing she noticed was that, except for her plain tailored white slip, she was stark naked!

Oh, Lord, surely she hadn't passed out while some poor woman flopped her dead weight around, tugging off her clothes! But then her ruined panty hose had come off at the hospital and been discarded, and she never wore a bra, being slender and firm enough not to need the support. So perhaps she hadn't put her hostess to all that much trouble, considering her button-front shirt and the wraparound skirt. It was embarrassing enough to have landed on the hospitality of strangers without that added indignity.

Careful of her throbbing head, she looked around her, taking in the obvious quality of the antique furniture, the pleasant mixture of periods, and fabrics in shades of blue and white with touches of persimmon. It was a feminine room. She silently complimented Mrs. Hamilton on her taste and then wondered why she instinctively felt that she wouldn't care for the woman.

Her husband, a true good Samaritan, was certainly nicer by far than any man Liza had known since her father. If he had seemed to cool down slightly after the hospital thing, then who could blame him? He had put himself to considerable trouble for someone who had more or less erupted into his life for a few rude moments and then dashed back out again...or at least tried to. He'd also no doubt been wondering what his wife would say when he brought home a strange woman at that hour of the night, along with an extremely pregnant dog.

Lady! Where was she? He had probably left her outside, considering her overall state of hygiene. By now she could be in the next county! Liza slid her legs gingerly over the side of the bed, discovering in the process that her left knee didn't want to bend and that her right elbow felt as if it were being bent backwards. She tottered to a door, opened it, and then closed it again. A closet with a pink raincoat and a pair of marabou-trimmed bedroom slippers.

Trying the next door, she discovered the bathroom. There she examined her reflection with growing distaste. She had never considered herself a beauty, for all her large, black-lashed blue eyes and pale, finely textured skin. She could have done with a smaller mouth and a longer nose—and without the handful of freckles. Now, transparently pale, with ghastly purple shadows beneath her eyes and a large, discolored area on her forehead, she looked like a fright mask. Her hair, a silky ebony crop that waved to her shoulders as a rule, was tangled and spiky and looked as if it had come with the mask. All she lacked was a peaked hat and a broomstick.

"Yuk!" She grimaced. "You'd better stay away from bonfires for a while, especially if there are any stakes nearby."

She washed the best she could without wetting the dressings on her knee and elbow. She was back in the bedroom searching for her suitcase when the door opened a crack. Thatcher Hamilton spoke softly from outside.

"You awake yet?" he inquired. Without waiting for her reply, he shouldered the door open and entered with a breakfast tray.

Liza stood frozen beside the Queen Anne high-boy, and they stared at each other silently for the longest moment she had ever known before she was jerked out of her trance by indignation. "You can't come in here!"

"I just did," her host said with quiet logic. "Now if you'll hop back in bed, I'll put this tray down. I hope you like scrambled eggs, because no matter how they start out, they always end up scrambled when I cook 'em."

Moving stiffly, Liza managed to get herself back into the bed and pulled the sheet protectively up over her chest. Not that there could be anything alluring about her plain white slip, but all the same ... a bed-room, a strange man, and her in her underwear, and darned little of that! "I could just as well come to the kitchen or wherever the rest of you are having breakfast. Honestly, Mr. Hamilton, I don't want to be any trouble for you."

She had an idea she had already caused more than a little trouble if he was having to cook and serve her breakfast. Slanting a look at him as he settled the wicker bed tray across her lap, she noticed once more that he was an extremely attractive man, even if he wasn't nearly as handsome as Todd. There was something ... reassuring, she thought, for lack of a better word, in the rugged construction of his features under a shock of rather unruly dark blond hair. The hint of gray that was threaded through it only added to his attractiveness. She noticed his strong, well-kept hands as he poured her coffee from a small silver pot. "It smells delicious."

"I *can* make good coffee, Liza," he allowed, straightening away from her.

"Hmm, ambrosial." She sipped appreciatively, acutely aware of his scrutiny as she avoided his glance. "My clothes," she mentioned hesitantly.

"Your suitcase is still downstairs. I left it while I settled your dog, and by then I was afraid you'd be asleep. The things you had on last night need a thorough scrubbing before they'll be wearable, I'm afraid."

She looked at him then, frowning earnestly against the growing pain in her head. "Oh, look, please don't let your wife go to any trouble on my account. All this—" she gestured to the tray and the room "—is too much, and I can't allow her to do my laundry, too."

"It's no trouble to throw them into the machine. When you're feeling more comfortable, we'll talk a bit, all right?" His words were hospitable enough, but there was something in his bearing that made Liza look at him doubtfully. Something in his tone of voice... or was it that he reminded her of someone she had met before, someone who remained stubbornly just out of reach in her memory? "Have we met before?" she asked him now, to be immediately startled by a look she could only describe as guarded. Then she told herself she was seeing things again.

A grin momentarily warmed his expression by several degrees before the frost came down again. "I think that's my line, isn't it, Liza?"

She shrugged, and that brought on an awareness of still more aches. Wincing, she asked him if he'd ever been to Chesapeake, Virginia.

"Not in at least several years," he admitted easily. So why did she have the impression that he wasn't being entirely frank with her?

Chalk it up to her own rather precarious condition at the moment. With a knot this size on her head, she'd be seeing leprechauns behind the door next!

"If you're still hungry, I can cook more eggs," he offered, and she realized that she had gobbled the whole plate full of eggs and bacon and toast in the few minutes he had been standing there.

"Oh, no. That is, no thanks," she said hurriedly, lifting the pot and pouring herself the half cup left in it. "I was just hungry, that's all. I'm fine now, honestly." Her large, clear blue eyes stared earnestly up at him, their effect only partly offset by the enormous shadows under them and the disfiguring bruise just above them.

"You didn't have dinner last night, did you?"

"Nor much lunch or breakfast either." She grinned ruefully.

His eyes dropped to what was visible of her creamy shoulders and the rather understated curves of her breasts. "You're not dieting, I hope."

"Nope. At least, not deliberately. I was in a rush yesterday morning and just had time to grab a cup of coffee before work and then, when I decided to head north, I packed a sandwich and an apple... only Lady wanted half my sandwich, as well as the core of my apple. From then on, things got sort of hectic," she finished with a smile that unconsciously appealed for a return to his former warm understanding.

Thatcher removed the tray from her lap, his hands brushing against her hips in the process. Only her acute sense of hearing made her aware of his sharply indrawn breath. She stared at him, openly perplexed. For some strange reason, she felt perfectly safe with him. Yet she knew herself to be as vulnerable as the next woman in the presence of a magnetically attractive man, and he was all of that. It was all she could do to remind herself that she was supposed to be in love with Todd.

"Yes, well ... maybe you'd better get another nap now, and we'll talk when you wake up. Your dog's been fed and watered and, unless I miss my guess, she'll be a mother before nightfall."

"Oh no! Just what I needed," she groaned. "Look, how'd you like to have a pet? Pedigreed roadhound, guaranteed female? You get six for the price of one," Liza added hopefully, perplexed at the slow hardening of his features. "No, I guess not. Wrong sort of neighborhood for girls of Lady's dubious morals. Oh well." She shrugged. "Can't blame a gal for trying."

Balancing the tray in one hand, Thatcher moved swiftly toward the door. "Sleep," he ordered tersely, but neither the tone of his voice nor the expression that looked uncomfortably like contempt was particularly conducive to rest.

Nevertheless, Liza lay back in the scandalously comfortable bed, musing on the way things had turned out. No longer did she feel the desperate uncertainty that had stricken her earlier. Not even the thought of Todd's fickleness had the power of arousing more than a slight twinge of disappointment, which was curious. She had loved him, hadn't she?

Or had she loved his stunning good looks, his suave manners, the careless and casual sophistication born of a lifetime of expecting the best of everything—and getting it?

Certainly she'd never encountered anyone quite like him before, at least not at close quarters. All the women in the store had flipped over him long before that day three weeks ago when he had strolled in wearing his tennis whites and ordered a cranberry red chiffon gown as easily as another man might order a ham on rye. Jerri Snow, the buyer, had known him for years. According to Jerri, Todd always bought his lovers parting gifts—the grande finale, she had called them. Shelly had been a little more blunt. "The kiss off. I knew this latest one wouldn't last long. Drinks like a fish, and even in Todd's set, a little of that goes a long way."

He had bought the dress, an Ann Klein and stunning, and three days later he had come in again and asked Liza for her home phone number.

"Why?" she'd asked, half drunk herself on his potent nearness.

"Because I'm going to be using it...quite a lot, starting from about five minutes after you get home from work today," he had purred suggestively.

Opening her eyes sometime later, Liza stared at the pattern of sunlight on the blue French wallpaper. It had lost its earlier brightness and now held a lemony tint that suggested a thin cloud cover. She groaned her way to her feet and crossed to the window, parting the brocade draperies to stare out over acres of wooded lawn that sloped down to the water. There were several out buildings and a circular driveway with a spur that led to what appeared to be a three-car garage. Just outside her window there was a beech tree, its leaves incandescent against the gray of the sky. It had been that that had filtered the weak sunlight, warming it slightly. Farther away, other beeches mingled with dark green pines and cedars and purpling sweet gums against the ruffled pewter surface of the water, and here and there, a persimmon tree offered its astringent fruit.

She was hungry again. No telling how many meals she had slept through. No one had come to wake her, and her watch had stopped at seven-forty-three. Still no sign of her suitcase. She'd have to complain to the management about the lousy service in this establishment. Meanwhile, bandages or no bandages, clothes or no clothes, she intended to have a shower.

Some twenty minutes later, dressed in a yellow silk robe she had found hanging on the back of the bathroom door, Liza set out to locate either her hostess, her host, or her suitcase, in no particular order of importance. If anyone objected to her informal appearance, that was tough. You'd think she was a prisoner or something.

Outside her bedroom door, she looked down a wide, pine-floored hallway to a window with an inviting-looking cushioned window seat. What a wonderful place to curl up with a book on a day like this. Several doors opened off the passage—bedrooms and baths, probably. Near one end, a banistered stairwell invited her to explore the lower portions of the house.

Her bare feet padded silently down the silky runner; she paused at the foot of the steps to stare around her. An older home, obviously, with all the delicious nooks and crannies that were no longer economically feasible. No sign of anyone around. She wandered through a wide doorway and found herself in an entrancing study, den, or drawing room—hard to tell which. It was furnished in softest grays with touches of gold and russet. An ancient Oriental rug set the color scheme, and it was picked up by the Jacquard weave on the sofa and the worn chintzes on a pair of large wing chairs. She recognized a rather baroque grand piano, its top covered with mounds of papers but there was no sign of a bench.

As soon as one idea of her host and hostess formed, it gave way to another. She wished someone would come and put her out of her misery. She couldn't very well leave in a borrowed negligee, and she hadn't the slightest idea where to start looking for her clothes.

One thing was certain. Neither she nor Lady belonged in a setting like this. More Todd's style. She'd been a fool even to hope she might find favor in the eyes of the Hardelys. A shopgirl. No background, no family, and most assuredly no money. They'd consider her a gold digger at the very least, and, come to think of it, didn't Todd owe her a farewell gift?

The idea struck her as hilarious and she giggled. She could picture him on Monday morning striding into Barnes and Taylor's fashion floor, ordering something in blue—chiffon, preferably—and as to size, his eyes would light on her replacement and he'd purr the familiar lines.

She lifted a hand to hold in the pain of her battered forehead as she laughed. When a gravelly, masculine voice unexpectedly sounded behind her, she gasped and spun around. A sharp pain flashed through her stiff knee. She lurched and would have stumbled had not Thatcher caught her by the elbows, which brought about a wail of agony.

He released her instantly with a grimace and then gripped her shoulders and steered her toward the sofa, pressing her carefully into its down-filled cushions. "For God's sake, what's wrong with you? Have you lost your mind?"

"I don't know, have you seen one lying around somewhere?"

He glowered at her. "If there's one thing I detest, it's a smart aleck."

"Sorry. We aim to please. Ooops, sorry again." Another giggle escaped her, and then to her consternation, her eyes blurred over and she was crying. Thatcher gathered her against him, and she buried her face in a sweater that smelled slightly musky and felt damp even without her own contribution. She cried for several minutes until she was able to choke off the tears again.

"It's those blasted pills," she muttered into his chest. "I took one of them a few minutes ago, and I'm not used to taking drugs."

"That's something, at least," he rumbled. Liza pulled herself away to frown up at him. His face looked all blurry and stern, and she blinked until she could see him more clearly.

"I don't seem to be making a very good impression as a guest around here, do I? If someone will just tell me where my things are, I'll hit the trail." There was something decidedly disturbing about the nearness of this big, hard man, and she was in no condition to cope with it at the moment. The sooner she put some miles between her and Thatcher Hamilton, the more secure she'd feel.

"Your suitcase is at the foot of the back stairs. I meant to take it up earlier, but when I checked on your mutt, I decided she needed prepping before maternity set in. She looks a hell of a lot better now, if none too happy about it. She was in shocking condition." His tone accused her, and Liza bristled defensively.

"Look, Lady and I met for the first time today... yesterday, that is, when she invited herself to lunch somewhere between the Severn River and the Bay Bridge."

He studied her until Liza felt herself blushing. Suddenly she was acutely conscious that she wore nothing at all under the crisp silk fabric of her borrowed robe. Embarrassment caused her to blunder into calling attention to that fact. "I... I borrowed this bathrobe. I couldn't find my clothes, and I was beginning to feel like a prisoner up there."

Thatcher continued to stare at her, but now his eyes moved to the primrose garment that was held together with a tied sash. There was nothing hurried about his scrutiny. It was a leisurely tour of all the possible points of interest, and Liza edged away from him.

"Look, if it's all the same to you...I mean, I don't want to offend you or anything, but I'd better be on my way. I have a long drive back home, and—"

"To 3-A Candlestone Apartments, Chesapeake, Virginia."

Her eyes widened, their clear blue somewhat clouded now behind her wet, matted black lashes. "How did you know that?"

"While you were being checked over in the hospital, I looked through your bag to find the necessary information for admission—name, age, address, social security number. Sorry if it offends your sense of privacy, but under the circumstances I had little choice."

"Oh, and I owe you for the bill. If you'll just let me have it, I'll—"

"I also know exactly how much money you have with you, Liza, and believe me, it's not enough to get you back home and pay your debts," he told her dryly.

"I'll send you a check as soon as I get home," she promised none too graciously. For some reason, Thatcher made her feel like a juvenile delinquent called before some higher authority. It was not a comfortable feeling, and for the life of her, she couldn't understand why it persisted. He had been the soul of kindness. Anyone else would have walked away rather than get involved in a stranger's misfortune.

As she stared at the figure of a golden dragon on the rug, he reached out and folded back the robe, baring her thigh. She gasped and pushed at his hand.

"Be still," he growled. "I see you were foolish enough to remove the dressing. I planned to wait until you saw the doctor this afternoon."

Biting her lip, Liza followed Thatcher's gaze to the scraped and bruised area of her knee. "Sorry," she muttered. "It's doing fine, though. I don't need to see the doctor again."

"You have an appointment at five."

"I can't afford to see the doctor again, as you very well know!"

"You'll do as I say, Liza. The cut could get seriously infected, and a little care now can prevent that from happening." His voice was stern, his eyes cool and slightly remote, but there was nothing at all cool or remote about the hand that was holding the calf of her leg. Hard, warm fingers pressed into the silky flesh, stroking as well as supporting. With her eyes still entangled with his, she jerked her leg from his grasp, wincing as the lacerated skin protested.

"Go get some clothes on!" he barked, moving swiftly to stand up. He was staring at her warily, as if he half expected her to reach out and pull him back down beside her, as if he didn't trust her for one minute. She frowned in bewilderment.

"Mr. Hamilton, I don't know what's going on here, but I think I'd better head for home. I... I promise you I'll see a doctor as soon as I get there, and I'll mail you a check and...and..." She frowned down at the yellow robe, disconcerted to discover that it had parted to reveal rather a large expanse of chest. She clutched it together and looked accusingly up at the man who towered threateningly over her. Why did he have to go and put ideas into her mind? Sex was the last thing she was interested in at the moment.

Or was it? Even in her indignation, she was far too aware of the powerful columns of his legs braced apart on the elegant carpet; the narrow, jean-clad hips that were bracketed by hard-looking fists, and the broad expanse of chest covered by a slightly moth-eaten sweater. He wore no shirt under it, and the sleeves were shoved up on his muscular forearms to reveal a coating of crisp hairs a shade darker than the mixed blond on his well-shaped head.

"Go put on your clothes, Liza. We'll talk over lunch."

Chapter Three

The familiar comfort of her favorite pair of jeans and a lavender pullover helped. At least, she didn't feel quite so vulnerable when she joined her host in the comfortable study. He was shuffling through the papers littering the top of the piano when she walked stiffly through the door, and he asked about her knee.

"Did you locate the bandages?"

"Yes, thanks. I feel a little like King Tut, but if I remember correctly from my roller-skating days, it's stiffest and sorest when it's healing over."

Thatcher favored her with one of his wintery smiles. "Something like that," he allowed.

Good Lord, why couldn't he thaw out? You'd think he'd uncovered her with her hand in the safe or something. "But I'm not going back to the doctor," she insisted.

Ignoring her, he gestured to a chair. "Sit down. Over here, where you can put your foot up."

Over here where the light will shine in my face, she thought rancorously, accepting his assistance to settle herself into the wing chair opposite the windows, with its matching ottoman. Not that there was all that much light coming through. It looked about five minutes short of a downpour.

Thatcher seated himself in a leather chair against a wall full of the bookshelves that extended on both sides of the tall windows. With his face in shadow, Liza was left with only her confusing impressions of the man. One minute he was all tender concern, the next he was being coldly judgmental, and then, for a fleeting moment, he radiated a purely masculine sexuality that made the blood race through her body with reckless speed.

"So...why don't you begin at the beginning, Liza Calahan, and tell me all about yourself?" he suggested. Oddly enough, even in ancient jeans and a sweater liberally sprinkled with dog hairs, Thatcher Hamilton looked perfectly at home in these quietly opulent surroundings. He had the sort of natural authority that made him stand head and shoulders above the crowd—any crowd. It occurred to Liza that Todd would shrink into insignificance before a man of Thatcher's caliber.

"Well?" he prompted, and she became embarrassingly aware that she had been staring.

"Sorry. I was thinking."

"Composing?" He lifted a thick eyebrow derisively.

"I don't know what you mean," she parried. But she did. For some reason, this man expected her to lie. Just how she knew that, she couldn't tell, but she was certain it was true. Feeling oddly defensive, she made a point of being scrupulously frank with him, even though it was none of his business. "As for what I'm doing here—I mean in St. Michaels—I came to spend the holiday weekend sailing with a...a friend."

"Male, of course," Thatcher put in dryly.

"I don't happen to know any females who own their own boat." Suddenly aware that her fingers were poking holes in the loose knit of her sweater, she forced herself to relax. "Anyway, it didn't work out. I mean, he...I..."

"Missed your connections? No, I'd say you connected, all right, only for some reason, you changed your mind at the last minute and decided to run out on him. What's the matter, Liza, weren't the stakes high enough?" He leaned forward to take a thin, dark cigar from a humidor on the coffee table, and pale gray light from the window played across the outline of his shoulders.

"I'm not sure just what you're getting at, but I don't think it's very flattering," she said cautiously.

"Pardon me. Did you want to be flattered?" He blew a thin stream of blue smoke into the room. Liza's head tilted with instinctive wariness.

"I don't want anything, Mr. Hamilton, at least not from you. And now, if you'll tell me where my dog is, I'll be on my way."

He didn't move. If anything, he seemed to settle deeper into the worn comfort of the rust-colored leather chair, exuding a sort of animal contentment. A distant furnace rumbled into action in the silence that seemed to echo around them, and as the wind picked up, a branch scraped noisily against the side of the house. The first few drops of rain hit the windows. Neither of them spoke. Liza eased her stiff knee from the ottoman and made an awkward attempt to stand. She winced. It felt as if someone were hammering on her knee from the inside.

"Sit down. Don't be so damned touchy, girl. It's nothing to me who you sail with or why. More to the point, is there anyone at home who needs notifying of your whereabouts?" He sounded impatient, as if weary of the whole affair. Liza would have given a month's rent to be on her way home.

Oh, would you now? a provocative alter ego taunted, and she stood there, swaying slightly as the hammers moved up to slam against her head. Thatcher was still seated, gazing up at her from the dimly lighted comfort of his chair.

"Sit down, Liza. You're not going anywhere, at least not today. Nor tomorrow either, and possibly not for some time."

"You're crazy! You can't keep me here!" Anxious, half-formed ideas filtered into her mind as she realized that she knew absolutely nothing at all about this man except for his name, and even that could be a lie. What if he were an impostor? What if he had broken into the real Thatcher Hamilton's home and was planning to hold her here . . . for ransom? That was too absurd, but there was still another possibility, one that made the headlines with depressing regularity, and his next words did little to tame the wild thoughts that seethed in her fertile imagination.

"So you've finally caught on, have you?" he sneered. "You're dead certain I'm going to lock you in the bedroom, rip off your clothes, and rape you. Go head, scream your head off. Who'll hear you?" He hadn't moved a muscle, and Liza could only stare at him, wondering which of them was insane.

"Oh, for God's sake, girl, have you taken a look at yourself lately? I'm not that hard up, believe me! Now, if you'll settle back down, I promise you,

you're in absolutely no danger from me. Somehow, I'll manage to control my baser masculine instincts."

If she hadn't sat, she would have fallen. She dropped limply back into the chair, leaving her burning, throbbing knee bent and both feet on the floor in case she should want to get up again in a hurry. Thatcher's eyes took her apart and put her back together again, and she cringed under the intense scrutiny.

"All right, suppose we go back to the beginning. You're from Virginia, right? You're on vacation. School? Job?"

She shrugged as if to say, What difference does it make? Then, with a reviving flash of spirit, she challenged him. "I'll tell all if you will. So far, all I know about you is your name, and I don't even have proof of that. At least you've seen my driver's license and my social security card."

"Have you any reason to believe I'm not who I claim to be?"

Eyes shifting uncomfortably, she muttered, "No...at least...well, no. But you'll have to admit, you're being pretty mysterious. So far I haven't even met anybody else in your family, and this doesn't look like a bachelor's pad to me, not even for a bachelor of your age."

In spite of the fading light, she caught his grimace. "Not that you're old," she amended hastily. Far from it. He was perhaps thirty-four or thirty-five and quite obviously in the prime of life.

"Thirty-four," he confirmed. "Lawyer by trade, specializing in maritime law, offices in Baltimore and Annapolis, currently vacationing at home of parents. Oh, yes...unmarried." He watched her as she digested the spate of information and then nodded her way. "Your turn."

"Where are your parents? I haven't seen a sign of anyone around here but you."

"My parents at this moment are probably somewhere in the Canary Islands. They're on a world cruise and I'm...I think the phrase is house sitting for them."

"But...who lives here? I mean, besides you?"

"You do, at the moment," he replied laconically. Liza took a deep, steadying breath and tried not to reveal how shaken she was by the implication of his words. Someone had undressed her last night, and she was awfully afraid it was this man.

He spoke again, as calmly as if he weren't aware of her agitation. "Your turn," he reminded her again.

"Oh." She swallowed a constricting knot in her throat. "Well, you know my name and age. I grew up outside Fredericksburg, moved to the Chesapeake area when I was thirteen, have lived there ever since. Parents both dead, no brothers, sisters, aunts, or uncles. No college degree and, at the moment, no profession. I'm...between jobs, you might say.'' She looked at him hopefully. Hoping for what, she couldn't have said. Acceptance?

''You might say,'' he repeated her last words thoughtfully. ''No family at all?''

Liza's gaze slid away, unwilling to delve into a past that was best forgotten. ''One stepmother, although I don't know if that relationship counts now that Daddy's gone. And anyway, what difference does it make? More to the point at the moment is how soon I can pick up my car and head home. After searching through my things, you know very well I can't afford to hang around here any longer. When I decided to come on this vacation, I expected to be someone's guest, and—''

''And aren't you?''

She frowned. ''Well, yes, but...well, not exactly. I mean, I really do appreciate everything you've done for me, Mr. Hamilton, but—''

''We won't go into that act again, if it's all the same to you. Let's consider something else. You say you're...between jobs. Does that mean you're in the market for employment?''

''Well, of course I am! I don't happen to be independently wealthy.''

"Can you do simple filing? Can you cook, keep house? Answer a phone and take a message with reasonable accuracy?"

Her mind a maze of doubts as well as a few totally unacceptable fantasies, she nodded. "I worked in an office once, but you may as well know I didn't last out a month. It's not that I didn't care for it, although I didn't especially. Personal problems, I guess you might say." Sexual harassment might be a more correct term, but there was no point in going into ancient history. That was why she had applied for the job selling women's fashions. At least there was no desk to be chased around, and fewer chasers.

Thatcher nodded thoughtfully, his long fingers steepled before his rather aggressive chin. It occurred to Liza irrelevantly that she'd hate to find herself on the opposing side of a court case from him. Neither of them spoke for several moments. Perhaps he was reconsidering his offer. As for Liza, she was fighting her impulse to grab that offer with both hands. Logic, of which she was lamentably short at times, told her she'd be crazy to take a job so far from home. Her apartment, Carol…there was every reason to refuse, and still she couldn't suppress the quiver of excitement that accompanied the idea of seeing more of Thatcher Hamilton, of working with him, even possibly living here in his parents' home with him.

Good Lord, the knock on her head must have addled her completely! She hardly knew the man, and she was all charged up at the idea of living with him.

"Made up your mind? Let me remind you of your responsibilities to your dog. She's in no condition to be moved at the moment, and the pups, when they come, will be in pretty sorry shape, I expect. She needed dosing, but at this late stage it wouldn't have been safe for either the bitch or her pups."

Common sense fought a losing battle with the rashest sort of feminine illogic, and she sighed. "I really shouldn't even consider it," she stalled.

"But you will. For the sake of my mother, as well as your dog, you will."

Abruptly, Liza stood and turned away, lifting a hand to stroke the knot on the side of her forehead. Her almost coltish grace unaffected by the stiffness of her limbs, she turned again to face him. "Why should you want to hire me? You don't even know me. You don't know a thing about my background except for what I've told you, and even that could be a pack of lies." She was half pleading with him to send her on her way, half afraid he would.

"I know more than you think, Liza Calahan. I know your stepmother, for instance. I attended your father's funeral, although we didn't meet at the time because I arrived late and left early to catch a plane. Corinne happens to be my first cousin, Liza. I recognized you almost at once, although you were only a child when I last saw you. So you might say we're related by marriage, and since we're both badly in need of a little assistance at the moment and I'm the closest thing you have to family other than your stepmother, who's somewhere on the West Coast, I think it's only fitting that we come to the aid of each other, don't you?''

Liza sagged into the chair, for once unaware of the discomfort of her battered knee. She couldn't have heard him properly. She must have misunderstood him. "Corinne Bradley?"

"Corinne Hamilton Bradley... Calahan. There's another one now, I believe, but as I haven't heard from her in a couple of years, I'm not sure just what it is."

"It's too wild," she protested. Something unpleasant had entered the atmosphere of the lovely old home with the mention of her stepmother's name, and she resented it. She desperately resented Corinne's cropping up to revive memories she had thought decently buried. "Are you sure?" she pleaded.

"I'm sure, Liza." His deep voice sounded almost bitter. It held less coolness, though, if little of the warmth he had revealed briefly the night before.

Liza wrapped her arms around her body, absently fingering the taped gauze on her elbow. Something in his tone, in the way he was looking at her, was distinctly unsettling. She felt as if she were wading in deep, uncharted waters, wondering with each footstep if the bottom was going to drop off under her.

"I do remember you, you know. You were what...thirteen? Fourteen? You were tall even then. Your eyes held a sad sort of innocence that made you look both older and younger than your years." He frowned and stubbed out his cigar in an alabaster ashtray, his movements jerky and somehow impatient. "You haven't changed as much as I'd have expected, all things considered," he said with a dry bitterness that puzzled her. "I don't have to tell you how worried Corinne was about you. She wasn't more than ten years older than you are now when your father died. A bit young and inexperienced to be landed with a juvenile—a teenager, that is."

Liza stiffened as remembered anger came over her. It had been a long time since she had last seen Corinne, and if she never saw her again, it would be too soon. The only time they had been in agreement about anything had been when they had gone home together after that last wretched meeting with the estate lawyers. Fred Calahan had had a small, highly successful construction company in King George County, Virginia, at one time. Within a year of his first wife's death, he had remarried, sold his business, and moved to Great Bridge, in the Chesapeake area. Urged on by his ambitious bride, he had bought an impractically large and expensive home in a showy new development and expanded his business enormously.

Liza had been sent off to school, and she had gone willingly. Corinne was the opposite of Rosalyn Calahan in all respects, and she made no pretense of caring for her newly acquired stepdaughter except when her husband was around. Being inherently honest herself, Liza had not been able to disguise her own resentment, and it had been better for all concerned for the family to split up. Summer school for three years in a row had put her close to graduation by the time Fred Calahan had had his massive fatal coronary. Liza would always believe it had been brought on by anxiety over his tremendous financial burden: the new home, an unfortunate recession in the building trade, and an extravagant new wife, not to mention Liza's own school fees.

They had made a pact that day. Corinne had inherited what was left of the meager estate after everything was paid off. The house, along with most of the other assets were in her name—for tax purposes, she had explained to the stunned teenage girl. Neither of them wanted to spend an unnecessary moment together, and so Corinne had agreed to pay Liza's expenses until she finished high school. Neither of them would notify the authorities that, to all intents and purposes, the child was unsupervised. Boarding school was out of the question, of course, but a two-room apartment was rented close to the local high school, and Liza managed quite well until at sixteen and a half she graduated with honors. She had all but given up hope of going on to the university to study architecture.

"Liza?" Thatcher summoned her quietly back from the past, his eyes searching her own until she looked away. "I think it will be best all around, at least until some of your bruises fade out. It'll be some time before you can face a prospective employer without inviting a lot of questions, and it'll give you time to reconsider your affair with your boyfriend as well. You might say I feel a certain amount of responsibility for your welfare."

Liza bristled instinctively. Sympathy was one thing, pity quite another, especially as it was mixed with something she couldn't quite put her finger on, something uncomfortably resembling censure. As if anticipating her rejection of his offer, Thatcher spoke up before she could answer him.

"The Chinese philosophy, remember? While I didn't exactly save your life by any stretch of the imagination, don't you think you owe me a few weeks of your time? I really am in dire need, you know." His smile was unfairly engaging. He had snapped on a tall table lamp, and the light emphasized the warmth she remembered in his hazel eyes. Liza felt the last barricade go down, and she knew with a sinking sensation that she'd be giving him more than a few weeks of her time before it was all over.

It was Lady who settled the last doubts. While Thatcher excused himself to go fix lunch for them, rejecting Liza's offer to take over the chore until she had recovered somewhat from her recent mishap, she went to visit the dog. Lady had been installed in a warm corner of the basement near the furnace. If Thatcher hadn't mentioned bathing her earlier, Liza might have had trouble recognizing her. She was still one of the homelier dogs she had ever seen, but her wiry coat now gleamed like dark wood, a mixture of black and reddish brown, and her tail thumped in welcome as Liza stretched out one stiff leg and lowered herself carefully beside the pile of clean burlap sacks.

Not until then did she notice the tiny wet bundle under Lady's foreleg, and even as she watched, another pup was born.

"Thatcher! Come quickly!"

He came within seconds. "What is it?" he demanded, drying his callused, masculine hands on an incongruously pink and white striped tea towel.

"It's started." Liza breathed in awe as still another of the tiny, wriggling things burst forth. Lady was busy bathing and nipping. When Liza looked up at the tall man standing beside where she squatted, there were tears running down her face, tears of which she was completely unconscious.

"Liza, Liza, it's all right, honey." Thatcher drew her up to stand beside him, careful of her knee and her elbow, and wrapped an arm around her shoulders.

Not trusting her voice for the moment, she could only avert her face, but he tilted her chin with his thumb and forefinger and laughed down at her gently. She couldn't possibly take offense. "I don't know what on earth is wrong with me," she managed finally. "I'm not usually so sloppy, I promise you." Her effort to laugh was not notably successful.

"I think I understand, Liza. Under the circumstances, it's only natural." He couldn't be aware of the effect his nearness was having on her. The momentary burst of emotion brought on by watching the process of birth had given way to feelings of quite another sort, and she was mortified for fear Thatcher would recognize them. The last thing she needed was for him to think she was attracted to him.

Five pups were born in short order, and that seemed to be the end of it. Liza refused to leave until Thatcher threatened to evict the lot. Then she reluctantly followed him to the kitchen. It was well into the afternoon by the time they finished lunch.

The next morning she was stiffer than ever, although most of the swelling had gone from her forehead. When Thatcher brought in her breakfast before she had managed to drag herself from bed, Liza complained loudly. "Look, this isn't going to work out. You say you need help, but you spend all your time waiting on me and my dog instead of lawyering, or whatever it is you're supposed to be doing. Why don't I just shove off today? Once I get my knee and my elbow bent at the proper angle, I should be able to make it to Virginia with no trouble."

"Eat your breakfast. If it'll make you feel any better, you can wash dishes and do the beds and anything else you feel up to doing. I'll be out all day, and I'll pick up something for dinner, so don't worry on that score."

Liza looked at him doubtfully over the wicker tray. This morning he wore tan corduroys and a rumpled gray pullover with a flannel shirt. There were patches on the elbows of the sweater and a few more places that should have been patched, and Liza wondered just how long he had been on his own. Impulsively she said, "You know, you look like a man who's been married for ten years whose wife has suddenly gone out of town."

"In other words, seedy."

"Definitely seedy," she agreed, breaking a piece of toast. She'd have to tell him tactfully that the toast should wait until the eggs were all but done. Better yet, she'd have to take over the chore of cooking herself.

"Believe it or not, I manage to look rather splendid when the occasion demands. Today, though, I'll be up to my knees in wood shavings, and I was always told that the mark of a well-dressed man is that he infallibly dresses for the occasion." Leaning in the doorway of her bedroom, arms crossed over his expansive chest, he looked disturbingly attractive, and Liza knew a sudden desire to run her hands up under that sweater and stroke the hard flesh beneath it.

She bent her head to her breakfast and mumbled through her toast, "I'll take care of things here. Is there a phone or something where I could reach you if anything comes up?"

"No. I'll check in sometime during the day. Take it easy. You're still not up to par, you know. I shouldn't have let you talk me out of taking you back to the hospital." Before she could protest, he went on. "If anyone calls, take a message, and tell them I'll get back to them before five."

Long after she had finished her breakfast, Liza leaned back against the down pillows and considered the unlikely situation she found herself in. Who could possibly have imagined a few days ago that she'd be having breakfast in bed in a late Georgian home on Maryland's Eastern Shore that made the fancy pseudo-mansion Corinne had insisted they buy look like a third-rate development house? Not only that, she had all but forgotten Todd, a man she had thought she was in love with when she had so recklessly raced off after him.

So much for her fickle attachments. Carol had accused her of being adolescent on more than one occasion, telling her she was afraid of allowing herself to get involved—which was no more or less than the truth. Liza had seen too many young girls get into serious trouble, even with the benefit of two parents. Knowing herself doubly vulnerable for being alone at fifteen, she had grown a set of defenses that didn't crumble easily, even now, when she was of age and living with a friend who was almost thirty. Besides which, socializing cost money, and she still harbored secret hopes of studying architecture, and that meant saving, hoarding every penny. Unfortunately, she was notoriously bad at holding a job and her decrepit automobile demanded more and more attention. As fast as she accumulated a nest egg, it went to buy a new fuel pump or a new set of recaps or some esoteric mechanical part that hadn't been manufactured in ten years.

The day passed uneventfully. There were no phone messages. Thatcher brought home fried clam strips, baked potatoes and limp slaw in throwaway plates. Over the next few days, Liza gradually lost all her stiffness, and the headaches did not return. Her coloring was still on the lurid side, but then, she spent little enough time studying her reflection in the mirror, and Thatcher seemed almost to avoid looking at her.

His attitude both puzzled and exasperated her. She could have sworn that there had been times when he was as aware of her as she was of him, but for all the attention he paid her now, she might be one of Lady's pups. In fact, the dogs came in for more of his concern than she did. He was talking of taking them to see a vet as soon as they were a couple of weeks older, and he checked the color of their gums carefully once or twice a day.

As for Liza, he couldn't have spent less time in her company if he'd deliberately tried. There were papers to be gone over each day at breakfast, and dinner, which she had taken over cooking, was eaten in the study while he watched a series of news programs. So much for gracious living. She had lighted candles in the dining room the first night and had prepared baked chicken, roasted potatoes, carrots, and a salad to go with it. She'd even made an effort to cover the worst of her bruises with makeup and arranged her hair over the rest. The one long dress she'd brought with her was a plum-coloured, washable satinlike material with a deep yoke of ivory net and lace topped with a high, stand-up collar of matching lace. Thatcher had taken one look at her as she brought in the platter of baked hen, and his face had visibly hardened. During the meal he'd barely spoken a word. In fact, it had almost seemed as if he'd avoided looking at her, and Liza had grown quietly furious.

She could wash his clothes and his dishes, cook his meals and make his bed, but other than that, she didn't exist for him!

No, that was not quite correct. Some of her anger was transmuted into a kind of hopelessness as she admitted to herself that she existed, all right, but it was as if his relationship with her stepmother put him into another generation. For the most part, he treated her with a kindly, if absent sort of condescension, as if she were a none-too-bright teenager.

With each passing day, she resented it more. She didn't know quite what it was she wanted from Thatcher Hamilton, but it was definitely not an uncle or a stand-in for her father.

Chapter Four

Several days later, Liza was curled up on the sofa with a set of blueprints she'd discovered under the reams of paper on the piano. Thatcher had warned her not to touch the precarious piles, informing her that it was thirty years' accumulation of his father's papers he'd promised his mother to go through and discard while they were away. Carstairs Hamilton, Thatcher's lawyer father, had had a stroke early in the year, and the cruise marked the end of his career and the beginning of his retirement. He had given up only with extreme reluctance, according to his son.

Liza had sailed through the room to answer the phone and accidentally brushed against one of the piles, scattering it onto the floor. She caught the phone on the fourth ring and answered breathlessly, "Hello, Hamilton residence."

After a long pause, a rather suspicious-sounding contralto demanded to know who was speaking. Liza gave her name and offered the additional information that Mr. Hamilton was not at home, but that she'd be glad to take a message.

"Just who are you, anyway? The maid? Housekeeper?"

"Both and neither."

"Exactly what does that mean?" the irritated female voice demanded.

"I think maybe you'd better ask Mr. Hamilton that," Liza suggested. "I'll be glad to have him call you when he gets home, if you'll leave your name and number."

After a pause that positively seethed with hostility and suspicion, the woman said, "Never mind!" and slammed down the receiver.

Liza shrugged. "Don't worry, I won't," she muttered as she turned to the task of clearing up the litter on the floor. It was then that she discovered the tantalizing sheaf of drawings. Leaving the rest of the mess where it had fallen, she picked up the blueprints, studying the topographical survey before turning to the next page.

An hour later she was still there, lost in a world she had all but forgotten. As a child, she had listened and watched while her parents talked and sketched and argued amicably over plans for the moderately priced homes for which Calahan Construction had been noted. Her father had custom designed each home, using unorthodox materials to advantage and surpassing the building codes to produce a home that would last for generations. There had been no cutting of corners, no standardization of style. Fred Calahan had tackled one building at a time, overseeing every detail and doing much of the labor himself, and had been able to make a comfortable living for his family as the quality of his buildings became recognized.

Liza had gone quickly from arranging toy blocks to using scrap lumber to knock together dollhouses. She had gradually discovered that she had a knack for clever design. All that had ended, however, when Rosalyn had suffered complications after a kidney operation and died within a week. When Fred Calahan had turned blindly for comfort to the attractive young divorcée who had come to work in the office shortly before Rosalyn's collapse, Liza had still been locked in her own world of grief. She had emerged months later to find herself on the outside as Corinne Bradley took over the running of her employer's home and his life.

A log settled noisily in the fireplace. Liza didn't even hear it. With the large blueprints spread over her lap, she lay back on the oversize sofa and stared up at the ceiling, as she had done as a child. Visualizing the uncluttered ceiling as a floor, her imagination took over and furnished the room with two wide doorways and four French windows and then went on to add a fireplace, bookshelves, a chair or two there, and a sofa here, with occasional tables and perhaps a piano. It did not occur to her before she fell asleep that she had merely refurnished the room as it was.

She didn't stir when the sheaf of papers was gently removed from her lap. When the cushions sagged beside her, she murmured softly in her sleep, and when something warm and firm touched her forehead, mingling with the warmth of her comforting dream, her arms lifted automatically to encounter the soft, woolly surface of a pair of broad, solid shoulders. In her dream, she gathered the comforting strength close to her.

"Liza, Liza, wake up, honey," someone breathed against her ear.

She didn't want to wake up. In the delicious half-world of sleep, she felt warm and protected and loving, and she turned her face to the source of that warmth. A groan sounded softly, and then her lips were covered and she became conscious of another set of sensations sweeping over her. Currents of electricity flowed down her body, short-circuiting her will to resist, even as she awoke to the realization that Thatcher was lying beside her, one of his legs thrown across hers on the accommodating sofa, his mouth on the heated softness of her throat.

She pressed her head deeper into the down-filled pillow to allow him free access, shuddering as chills triggered by the delicate touch of his tongue searching out every nerve ending coursed down her side. There was no question of withdrawal in her mind. Floating slowly up from a dream world in a sea of pure sensation, she was incapable of any thought at all, much less of making a conscious decision concerning the wisdom of her actions. She slipped her hand under Thatcher's sweater, and he lifted himself long enough to tug the garment impatiently over his head. Her fingers made short work of the buttons of his flannel shirt, and soon she was combing through the pelt of body hair on his muscular chest, tracing the pattern of ribs under the flat sinews, stroking the swell of his powerful pectorals. Her fingertips encountered the hardened pinpoints there, and a bolt of lightening shot through her at his physical reaction to her touch.

"Oh, God, this is crazy," he groaned, but when she lifted her mouth to shut off his words, he ground his lips against hers, thrusting aggressively with his tongue as he positioned her even more intimately against him.

She felt as if her very bones had turned to liquid gold, flowing hot and brilliant through her body. The air shimmered around them. When his hand moved under the loose cover of her sweater to find her breast, she trembled uncontrollably. He whispered her name over and over in husky, agonized tones, and the sound registered on every segment of her spinal column. "Make me stop, Liza. I can't do this to you... not to you, of all people... but God help me, I've wanted you from the first moment I saw you."

She laughed softly, glorying in the feeling of unaccustomed power over him. "Not the first moment, surely. I was only a child, remember?"

He lifted himself to stare down at her, and she searched his face for a clue to his thoughts. Desperately she sought to enter his mind, to discover the essence of the man who was Thatcher Hamilton. His eyes were unrevealing rings of green gold circling unnaturally large dark pupils. "Do you think I don't know that?" he grated out. As he swung his legs off the sofa, Liza caught at his arm.

"Don't go," she begged softly, half shyly.

She flinched from the withering look he cast over his shoulder. "Pull your sweater down. You look like a tramp!"

The cold war lasted for two days. If it hadn't been for Lady and her babies, Liza would have packed up and left, although she was not willing to admit, even to herself, what leaving Thatcher would mean to her. One of Lady's pups seemed to lag behind the others. Liza had been offering supplementary feedings, willing the small handful to hang on until he was old enough to be treated by a vet. Perhaps it was the lack of anyone of her own to love that made the canine family so precious to her. After all these years of holding herself slightly aloof, of guarding against the vulnerability of allowing herself to love, she'd been unable to resist the appeal of the hapless mongrel and her clutch of babies, most of whom resembled teddy bears at the moment.

Lady's trusting amber eyes watched her every move as she held the runt up to her face, inhaling the pungent, but not unpleasant odor common to puppies. Her mind drifted on the prevailing currents. What was she going to do about Thatcher? He'd apologized to her last night at dinner, speaking with the slightly stiff formality he resorted to more often than not, as if he were a legally appointed guardian and she were still a minor, she thought bitterly.

Lord knows, she didn't feel very minor where he was concerned. If she had her wits about her, she'd be three hundred miles away at this very moment. Instead, she allowed a foolish attachment for a stray hound to serve as an excuse to keep her here. At least she no longer tried to delude herself about the real attraction. If an almost compulsive desire to throw herself into Thatcher's arms, coupled with a growing feeling of trust and respect, plus an insatiable desire to win his admiration, added up to the total she suspected, then she was dangerously close to being in love.

"So how can I make him see me as a woman and not just the gawky stepdaughter his first cousin was saddled with?" she asked the small bundle of fur in her hands. If just once he'd let himself go, if she could break through that hidebound set of rules that went along with his lofty calling and his strong sense of family, she might be able to make a dent. As it was, except for that one occasion when he'd found her asleep and tried to awaken her gently, he had treated her with a distant sort of kindness, finding less and less time to be with her except for mealtimes or the few minutes a day it took to go over his mail, not that he allowed her to help him with it. For all she knew, his business mail went unanswered, unless he had a secretary stashed away somewhere in town.

She replaced the pup, allowed her hand to be bathed by his mother, and wandered slowly up the stairs into the kitchen. Of course, it might be that he simply didn't fancy her. She was nothing to write home about, after all—features too irregular to be called pretty, body too lanky to be considered cute.

As for education and experience, she fell far short of being his equal, and he probably found her a singularly uninteresting companion.

On the other hand, there had been no disguising the fact that he had been as aroused by her as she had been by him that night on the sofa. Of course, he'd caught her off guard, and one thing had led to another. Physiology being what it was, few men would have reacted differently, but all the same, he wasn't completely indifferent to her. That was something to build on perhaps. Maybe she'd have to plot a deliberate campaign—capture his body, intrigue his mind, then go to work on his heart, she told herself, only half jokingly. The only trouble was, she hadn't the slightest idea how to go about it.

By the end of her first full week as housekeeper, cook, message taker and paper sorter, she knew little more about Thatcher Hamilton than she had the first day. He took his coffee black, his eggs soft, his oysters raw. He liked Shostakovich, Berlioz, and Aaron Copland, deplored the increasing trend toward jargon, and had turned to hunting with a camera instead of a gun in spite of a fondness for roast duck. She still had only the vaguest idea of how he spent his days, other than that his firm was planning to open an office in Easton sometime in January of next year. She could only assume he spent his days doing something in connection with that. Her first few inquiries had been neatly sidestepped, and pride had prevented her from persisting.

When the doorbell sounded, she had just stepped out of the shower. Biting her lip, she stood in the middle of the bathroom, a towel draped around her head. Who on earth could it be? Certainly not Thatcher. He used his key, and besides, it was not time for him to be home yet. Wrapping the yellow silk robe around her, she skipped down the stairs barefooted and peered through the beveled glass panel beside the door. The sight of the woman who stood tapping her booted foot impatiently was both reassuring and disquieting. She opened the door cautiously.

"Well, it's about time!" came a vaguely familiar contralto before Liza could utter a sound. Without waiting to be invited inside, the woman pushed open the door and strode in, turning abruptly to survey Liza with a pair of cold eyes that were set like gray agates in a flawless face. "Would you kindly tell me what you're doing here in Thatcher's house wearing my clothes?"

Overcome by a dryness of the mouth that extended to her brain, Liza could only stare. Her small store of self-confidence began rapidly to crumble at the edges as she fingered the sash of the robe and stared at the classical perfection of the rigid face before her. "I . . . uh . . . won't you come in?" she stammered, backing away and gesturing to the study that was used as a living room.

"I don't need any invitation from you!" the older woman declared. She was somewhere in her early thirties, intimidatingly well groomed in gray suede boots and a camel tan suit over a gray cashmere sweater, with her honey blond hair worn in a smooth pageboy style. "Where's Thatcher? You obviously failed to give him my message!"

Biting back an angry retort, Liza willed herself to proceed cautiously. Whoever the woman was, regardless of her lack of good manners, she was certainly confident of her right to be here. "You didn't give me any message."

Glacial eyes bored into her own as if the older woman willed her to perdition. It was all Liza could do not to dash up the stairs and slam herself inside her room—only that, too, probably belonged to the self-assured creature, considering that that was where the robe had been hanging. Damn Thatcher Hamilton! He could have warned her, at least. "Look, I'm sorry if there's been some sort of misunderstanding between—"

"Oh, please!" drawled the other woman with exaggerated patience. "The only misunderstanding is on your part. Thatch is well known for collecting strays, but as a rule, he has better sense than to give them the run of the place. I've warned him time and again that one of these days he'll regret his misplaced generosity. But then, most men lack judgment in certain matters," she finished with a bitter snort of laughter.

Adopting an attitude of disdain that was sheerest bravado, Liza said, "So I've noticed, but then, it's different when it's family."

The blonde stalked across the muted Oushak rug, tossing her pigskin gloves and a silk scarf on a chair before pouring herself a glass of Thatcher's sherry. Liza couldn't help but think that if the woman had tried to dress for the setting, she couldn't have done better. "Oh," the other purred, turning to stare with growing speculation at Liza standing hesitantly in the doorway. "The Corinne thing. He mentioned picking up a girl who had some remote connection with his cousin, but, of course, I thought you'd have the good manners not to impose on his misplaced hospitality."

Oh, did you? Liza mused silently. She rather thought not. This woman had obviously come to investigate Thatcher's houseguest and was none too pleased with what she'd found. The thought gave Liza small satisfaction. "If you'll excuse me, I'll go put on some clothes," she murmured, backing toward the stairs. She'd certainly never wear the yellow robe again, if she had to drape herself in a bedsheet!

"Yes, do that. Not that I'll be wanting my robe back. You may take it with you when you go. It's raw silk, not polyester, by the way, so don't throw it in the washer."

As if I couldn't be expected to recognize the difference! Lord help me to hold my tongue and keep me from braining the creature, Liza muttered silently as she climbed the stairs to her bedroom. If there was one thing that got under her skin, it was condescension. Corinne had had a way of making her feel incredibly inept, gauche, stupid, and ugly, and since then there had been a few occasions at the store when someone had tried the Lady-Bountiful-to-lowly-shopgirl routine on her. Now, considering her precarious position in the Hamilton household, it was hardly surprising that someone as beautiful and self-assured as the blonde downstairs sipping Thatcher's best blend of sherry should have a disconcerting effect on her.

She took her time pulling on her jeans and tugging the loose-knit lavender sweater over her head. On the verge of stepping into her shoes, she fell across the bed and propped her chin thoughtfully on her fists. It was beginning to look as if she might be on the road again before the day was over. The pups could be bundled into a box and driven back to Virginia with her, and she'd manage to sneak them in somehow. Carol wouldn't care. In fact, Carol would probably be more upset to see Liza than the dogs. No doubt she had already installed her steady boyfriend in Liza's space, which suited Liza fairly well, considering Hank was a far better housekeeper than Carol was. The two of them had been picking at the idea of taking an apartment together for months now, anyway.

All of which skirted the real issue. There was no avoiding the fact that the woman downstairs was someone special as far as Thatcher was concerned. He had told her about Liza and about her connection with Corinne. The idea of his discussing her behind her back with anyone rankled, but especially with Princess Iceberg! The woman had come hotfooting it over here just as fast as she could manage, to protect her own interests—as if Liza were any real threat to someone with her looks and obvious breeding.

Maybe it was a good thing, after all, she mused balefully. She had actually begun to dream, to hope, to build on the occasional flash of physical awareness he had shown.

More than awareness, she recalled wryly. If he hadn't caught himself in time the other night, they'd both have been beyond the point of no return. In all her twenty years, she'd never been so affected by a man. If that meant she was in love, then the sooner she got out of here, the better. One more such occurrence and she'd be hooked, and a fat lot of good that would do her!

She heard the distant slamming of a car door. That would be Thatcher. He let himself in quietly, and then she heard the hum of voices drifting up the stairwell outside her door. May as well stay here, let them get it all out in the open. She could predict the course of events.

Darling, the blonde would exclaim, why on earth did you allow yourself to be saddled with that impossible creature? She was unbearably rude to me, not to mention borrowing my things without my permission, and there's certainly no obligation on your part to take her in off the streets. She's Corinne's responsibility, not yours.

Oh yes, Liza could predict the course of the conversation with ease. It would take about ten minutes, only part of which would be spent talking, no doubt, before Thatcher would come upstairs and invite himself in to have a little talk with her.

The rap on her door, when it came, startled her nevertheless. She had been playing a childish game with herself—imagine the worst and it won't happen.

"Liza? May I come in?"

"It's your house." She didn't bother to get up or to turn and look at him when he closed the door quietly after him. She could sense his presence. The whole room vibrated with it. It occurred to her then that he wouldn't be a stranger to this room, not when his girl friend had felt free to leave some of her things behind. The thought of their intimacy twisted something inside her painfully, and her fists clenched beneath her chin.

"Will you get up, or shall I join you there?" he asked, amusement running under the rough surface of his voice.

She rolled over and scrambled to her feet, her large eyes accusing in spite of her vow to remain unemotional. "Well?" she challenged when he continued to study her features. She resented the unexpected tenderness she found there. It was as if he knew how she felt and was already regretting the necessity of hurting her, of sending her packing.

"Why didn't you come on back downstairs after you changed?"

"Is there any reason why I should?" She hated her own flippancy. It bordered on rudeness, but she couldn't help herself.

"Not if you don't want to, of course, but you can't stay up here forever. Besides, I thought we'd go out to dinner tonight. There's a place that serves—"

"You go. Take your... your lady friend. I'm sure she'll enjoy it. There's no reason for me to tag along. After all, it's not as if I were—"

"Stop sulking, Liza," he ordered softly. "I invited Ilona here mostly for your benefit, you know."

"For my benefit! Well, thanks, but no thanks. I can do without being made to feel like a cockroach in the pantry!"

He grinned disarmingly. "That's a pretty graphic description. I think you're imagining things, child."

"Oh, do forgive my misunderstanding," she said, her voice dripping sarcasm. "And for your information, I'm not a child!"

He sobered, his eyes dropping swiftly to the gentle swells that lifted the soft knit of her sweater. "Which is precisely the reason I invited Ilona to stay with us, Liza. I...in spite of my good intentions, I don't think it's particularly smart to invite...well, speculation. It won't do your name any good to be living here unchaperoned with a man—a single man."

Willing away an upsurge of tears—it was pure frustration that made her feel like hitting out blindly at something or someone—she said, "Are you worried about my good name or yours? No one even knows me in this part of the country, but maybe your reputation couldn't stand it. Maybe it isn't the first time you've dragged home some girl you picked up. According to your girl friend, you make a habit of it." Her voice was beginning to sound high and unsteady, and she finished in a spurt while she could still manage to control it. "Tell me, does she always rescue you before you get in over your head? How wonderfully forbearing of her!"

The full lower lip that could look so sensual at times was nowhere in evidence as Thatcher skewered her with a look of utter contempt. His mouth was hard, the planes of his lean cheeks more pronounced than ever. Liza shuddered involuntarily, but she didn't lower her eyes. It was as if she hung limply suspended from the very strength of his disapproval.

"If you've quite got it out of your system now, we'll go downstairs and you can apologize to Miss Clark."

The forbidding image wavered before her as her vision clouded, but Liza opened her eyes still wider to accommodate the sudden moisture. "I don't consider I owe Miss Clark an apology. I didn't have more than half a dozen words to say to her, and none of those were really...really what I felt like saying," she admitted, finally dropping her gaze. He knew exactly what she felt like saying, of course. She'd just said it all. If she owed anyone an apology, it was Thatcher. She stepped back, bumping against the bed. Making a valiant effort, she began. "Thatcher, if I—"

"Liza, Liza," he interrupted, his tone rueful as he brought his hands up to clasp her shoulders. He shook her gently, and at his touch Liza fought back a subliminal vision of the two of them together on those pale blue sheets. She stiffened instinctively, pulling away, but he held her fast. "Liza, please try to understand. I want you here. I . . . well, you might say I feel responsible for you."

"The old Chinese thing?" she flung at him disparagingly, but he shook his head, his hazel eyes warming and crinkling at the outer corners.

"No, not the Chinese thing. Liza, I told you I remembered you from your father's funeral. I did. I do. When Corinne got in touch with me a few weeks after that to tell me . . . well, we won't go into that now. I'm sure you'd sooner forget the whole painful episode, but you may as well know that I'm aware of what went on about that time. Corinne turned to me as family, because she couldn't swing things alone, and her parents weren't in a position to help out. I offered what help I could, and I assumed everything turned out satisfactorily—as satisfactorily as something of that sort ever can, that is. I know you're not particularly fond of my cousin, but believe me, she did what she considered best under the circumstances. The very fact that you're obviously getting along fine, with a life of your own, leads me to believe she took the right step. Any alternative would have been . . . difficult."

Liza sagged in his hands as she rejected the whole painful episode of the last grim scene between her and her stepmother, when she'd accused the older woman of stealing first her father and then her inheritance. She supposed she should consider herself fortunate that Corinne had agreed to pay her expenses while she finished high school. According to her, there was not that much left, and not until much, much later did it occur to Liza to wonder what had happened to her own mother's things. By then, Corinne was long gone, and she herself was installed in a two-room apartment with cheap plastic furniture and fake paneling that sagged out from the walls. It would have broken her heart to see her mother's rosewood and velvet loveseat, her inlaid sewing table, and her collection of cranberry glass in such surroundings.

"Friends?" Thatcher queried gently, raising her face to the merciless rays of the late afternoon sun that flowed in through the open draperies.

Friends! "I'll try," she managed. Try to hold back the intensity of her feelings, to force them into the smaller, less demanding mold.

He almost undid all the good work, though, when he moved his hands from her shoulders to clasp her face. When he lowered his lips to kiss each cheek just below her eyes, she caught her breath in a shuddering gasp. Only when he removed the warmth of his mouth and she became aware of the cool wetness did she realize the tears she thought she'd controlled so admirably had finally betrayed her by overflowing.

As it turned out, she was allowed her way, after all. Thatcher took Ilona Clark out to dinner, while Liza stayed at home and dined on cold ham and watermelon rind pickles. She went down to the basement and sat beside the dogs for perhaps three-quarters of an hour, appreciating their undemanding companionship. Oddly enough, she didn't worry about her future in the Hamilton household, Ilona or no Ilona. It was as if her mind had simply turned off. She had no say in her future at this point, nor did the fact bother her, oddly enough. After years of making her way, of keeping her own counsel, studying, working, and getting by, she was content just to drift. Tomorrow would be soon enough to engage her brain again.

The worst that could happen to her was that she'd find herself headed back to Virginia once more, and after all, she'd never planned to stay in Maryland for more than a few days. She knew from past experience that when something hurt too much, a sort of numbness came down over her to block out the pain. If leaving Thatcher behind was like amputating a part of her, then she'd weather it. She'd lost someone before and recovered, and any scars were well hidden from view.

After a while she went upstairs and crawled into bed, giving not a single thought to where the other guest would sleep.

Chapter Five

If it was difficult on Liza's part to accept Ilona Clark's presence in the household, she had the dubious pleasure of knowing it was even harder for the older woman. Liza reluctantly agreed to accompany her on an inspection tour of the house—"Just to be certain everything is just as Jean left it."

Thatcher was meeting with a workman about a boat of some sort. He didn't volunteer any details, and since Ilona obviously knew all about whatever boat it was, Liza's stiff-necked pride would not allow her to reveal her own ignorance.

"Jean is so particular about her things, but, of course, a man will take the easy way out. And while I'm sure you've done your best, my dear, you don't mind if I have a look around?'' The older woman bared her perfect teeth in a facsimile of a smile, while her cold North Atlantic eyes slid disparagingly over Liza's worn jeans and shapeless sweater.

Liza made a mental note to call Carol the first chance she got and have some of her clothes sent on. She probably wouldn't be around long enough to benefit, but while she was here she could do without that particular handicap. At least her brief time at Barnes and Taylor had taught her a few things about clothes, and she'd been amazed to find herself in growing demand as a model for small in-house showings.

Feeling much as she had the day she'd first reported for work in the fashion department wearing a chain-store cotton dress and flat sandals, she followed Ilona through the large, beautifully kept house. They were in the formal living room, and the older woman opened another door and glanced through to a smaller sitting room that was distinctly feminine in flavor. ''This, of course, is Jean's hideaway. Thatch prefers his father's study, but I believe this one can be made into something we could both enjoy.'' She stood there as if lost in thought, and Liza stared at her in growing dismay. Did that mean what it sounded like?

''I don't understand,'' she began hesitantly. ''Aren't the Hamiltons planning to return?''

Ilona turned with a show of confusion, her cashmere skirt swirling nicely around her small, curvaceous legs. She was half a foot shorter than Liza, and every inch of her very feminine frame was flawlessly and expensively groomed. "Oh dear, am I letting the cat out of the bag? Well, strictly *entre nous,* Thatch has recently bought up an old property on the river... but, of course, he'll have told you all about it." She smiled sweetly. "The one I'm helping him remodel for his offices." Wandering about the room, she touched first one thing, then another, her short, pink-tipped fingers lingering in an unpleasantly possessive manner. "There's plenty of room left over for a lovely apartment, and since both Car and Jean have a ridiculous thing about servants—Jean insists on doing most of her own housework—we thought the smaller place might be perfect for them. This house needs complete redoing, anyway. It has absolutely no flavor."

"I think it's lovely as it is," Liza said, defensive on behalf of the handsome old brick house.

"Oh well, of course you would. To someone of your background—I mean no offense, my dear, but let's be frank—this is hardly what you're accustomed to, now is it?" She closed the door on the chilly formal room and turned to the dining room, with its faded mural and softly gleaming china, crystal, and silver behind beveled glass doors. Running a hand over the slightly dimmed surface of the mahogany table, she shook her head. "Too old to be good, not old enough to be antique. All this was just the thing when Car and Jean furnished the place, but that was aeons ago. Lord, can you imagine, they came here when they were first married and have lived here ever since! Tell me honestly, do you know anyone else who hasn't moved at least once? Old family properties are great, but believe me, I was never more relieved than when I was able to move out of my parents' mausoleum and into my own place in Roland park."

They toured the bedrooms. Ilona had insisted on Liza keeping the blue room. "I always used it before, but then I can just as well take the master bedroom. It will give me a chance to decide what changes I'll want to make there."

Thatcher joined them for lunch, a lunch that Liza had prepared after Ilona had disclaimed any interest in taking over the domestic side of the household. "Be my guest, darling. I don't happen to share Jean's hangup about servants. You may cook for me to your heart's content."

Thatcher strolled into the dining room, still wearing a flush of outdoors on his tanned features, and Liza noted Ilona's quick frown at his casual attire. "*Bay Bird*'s been hauled, scraped, and copper painted," he said, "and I'm thinking of having them go ahead and repaint the trim when they do the interior. Does your training cover boats?'' He grinned at Ilona as he helped himself to a serving of Liza's corn chowder. Turning to the younger woman, he said, ''I guess Ilona told you she's an interior designer. I've prevailed on her to give me a hand with my new offices. This is great soup, by the way. What's it seasoned with?''

Busy reshuffling her ideas as to the purpose of Ilona's visit, Liza stared blankly at him and then murmured, ''Hmm? Oh...tarragon, mostly. Bacon, onions, tomatoes, corn and—''

''My dear, Thatch could hardly be interested in the complete recipe,'' Ilona broke in, leaning across the table to touch the back of his hand lightly. ''If you want my suggestion about the sloop, how about a rechristening? *Bay Bird* sounds so...banal. Why not something a little more personal?'' She waited, with a look Liza could only describe as coquettish on her face, while Thatcher ignored her and applied himself to his lunch. With a swift frown that was as swiftly erased, Ilona changed the subject. ''I have scads of samples in the back of my car. Why don't we run into Easton for a preliminary survey as soon as we finish lunch? I've never even seen the place, you know. Only for you, you ungrateful wretch, would I allow myself to be rushed blindly into something of this sort.''

It was several hours before they went to town, however, and when they did, Liza accompanied them, to Ilona's obvious displeasure. After lunch, Thatcher had wanted help in going through his mail, and Liza had stacked the dishes hurriedly while Ilona stalked away to place a phone call. "While you may not value my services so highly, darling, others do," she had told Thatcher sullenly. "Lord knows why I let you talk me into running out on my other clients."

While Thatcher shuffled through his briefcase in search of something or other, Liza quickly sorted the accumulated mail into three piles: personal, business, and junk. Sitting primly on the sofa, she said, "If you're not particularly interested in investing in mail order diamonds or in having the house redone in aluminum siding, I'll file these away in the circular file."

He looked up and grinned, having extracted a sheet of what seemed to be building specifications. "Next case."

"A card from someone named Rich." That provoked a frown, and she apologized hurriedly. "The message was so short I read it before I realized what I was doing."

"Well?" he prompted impatiently.

"Anon."

"What?" he growled impatiently.

"'Anon.' That's all it said. Just 'Anon,' Rich. There's a lovely picture of the Ford Theatre on the other side."

"Let's get on with it. File that one with the diamonds and siding."

There was another, rather more informative card, from the elder Hamiltons. "Rock of Gibralter still solid. We're both doing fine, eating too much, getting too much sun, and missing St. Michaels. Please water *all* the house plants when the shamrock leaves droop. It's my barometer."

Thatcher smacked a hand against his forehead. "Damn! I forgot."

"Don't worry, I found them. Your mother put them in her own sitting room, where it's cooler. They weren't too far gone, and all but the potted eucalyptus will pull through."

"Thanks. Anything else?" He took the sheaf of business letters from her and leafed through them before tossing them aside. "If you've got a dress, go climb into it. I thought we'd make an evening of it, since we'll be in town anyway. Give you a break from your chores." His smile was warm in an absent sort of way—altogether too attractive. Liza closed the door and leaned against it for a moment before dashing upstairs to look over her skimpy wardrobe. His reaction to her plum-colored satin had not been particularly encouraging, not that it would have been suitable for traipsing around in an unfinished office building, anyway. No doubt the impeccable Miss Clark would come up with the perfect outfit to bridge the gap between work and dinner.

Hearing Ilona in the front bedroom, Liza moved the hall extension to the jack in her own room and dialed Carol, surprised when her apartment mate actually answered.

"Hi, it's me. Look, Carol, could you possibly mail me some clothes? I'm here with exactly three outfits, and one of those is that long satin thing!"

After promising faithfully to send on as much as the post office could handle, Carol went on to confirm the rumors they had both heard of the apartment owner's plan to turn the building into condominiums before the end of the year. They exchanged impressions of the sort of money-grubbing worm who would do a thing like that to his unsuspecting tenants, and Carol promised to keep her posted on developments.

"Just what I need, one more complication," Liza muttered as she slumped on the blue velvet slipper chair and glared at the inoffensive phone. After a moment's hesitation, she dutifully took it back out to the hall, despite the fact that there were at least two phones on the second floor.

Just after four o'clock, Thatcher called upstairs that he was ready to head for Easton. Ilona had been with him in the study when Liza had remembered the dishes and dashed down to finish up in the kitchen. Hearing the low murmur of voices, she'd gone back upstairs to her room. A little of Ilona Clark's malicious looks and patronizing tones went a long way, and Liza was no glutton for punishment.

Her few garments looked lost in the spacious closet. It would have to be the white skirt again. At least she had the consolation of knowing she wore clothes well, even if the clothes themselves weren't quite the thing for dining in town. No doubt Ilona would insist on going to someplace swank and expensive. One could hardly imagine her sitting before a stack of old newspapers wrestling with hard-shelled crabs while the juice dribbled down her elbows.

Applying a glaze of berry red to her full lips, Liza tilted her head to examine her reflection. There had to be something there. Todd had not been the first man to pay attention to her. She'd been on the receiving end of some pretty strong flattery from other sources as well, but whatever her appeal, it escaped her completely. Her face was bony, her cheekbones too pronounced, her mouth too large, and her nose far short of elegant. Her front teeth, while pearly enough, were a bit too large to suit her, too. Perhaps it was her eyes. The long, thickly black lashes contrasted with the blue irises, turning them into something a little out of the ordinary. Maybe she should learn to bat them around. She attempted a modest flutter.

"Liza, if you're waiting for a trumpet fanfare, forget it!" Thatcher called up the stairway. She voiced a mild oath, grabbed her purse, and dashed down to where the others waited.

Ilona, of course, looked ravishing in a belted Russian broadtail coat. The weather was not nearly cold enough for fur, and Liza hoped she smothered before the evening was over. Of course, a woman like Ilona Clark was constitutionally incapable of perspiring.

Seated alone in the back of the Mercedes, Liza wrapped her white acrylic cardigan more closely around her and glared at the back of Thatcher's head. Even from the back he looked unfairly handsome. The very angle of his well-shaped head spelled authority, command, and a natural superiority few men she had met could compete with.

Phooey! I'm not all that easily impressed, she assured herself. There are far more important things in life than money and position. She refused to listen to the whisper that reminded her that money and position were the very least of his attractions.

The building Thatcher had bought to house his new offices—and an apartment for his parents, according to Ilona—sat on several acres of bulkheaded riverside. There were large pines and a variety of hardwood trees along the waterfront, and the house must once have been stunning. Even now, with debris from the half-finished restoration very much in evidence, its personality was powerful. Square, two-storied, with a cupola on top and a number of bay windows, it rested comfortably among the surrounding oaks, wearing its gingerbread trim like a lace collar and cuffs.

"I've had storm windows put over the stained glass. It was so old it was crumbling. Older than the house itself, I suspect." Thatcher had come to stand beside Liza while Ilona collected books of paint and fabric samples from the trunk of the car.

"It's beautiful, Thatcher. Don't you wish it could have kept a diary all these years?"

His nice eyes sparkled down at her, and then he frowned. "You're shivering. Come on inside, although it'll probably be even worse in there. The ductwork for the heat isn't finished yet."

He led her inside and then went back to help Ilona bring in her samples. Liza wandered through the empty rooms, her arms wrapped around her body against the damp cold and her footsteps echoing on the hardwood floors. Thatcher joined her just as she came to a newly painted door with far more sophisticated hardware than the old porcelain knobs and skeleton keys used in the rest of the house.

"Here we are. Come on inside and tell me what a marvelous job I've done on the cabinets," he invited, unlocking the door and allowing both women to pass through.

They spent a long time in the four rooms that comprised the office suite. The walls, for the most part, were stark white plasterboard. "I left the paneling where I could, but most of these partitions are new, and one wall had to be completely reconstructed. I saved the original wood and used it on the cabinets. Heart pine, most of it," Thatcher told them. Ilona had spread her samples out across the gleaming surface of a counter that ran under a wall of bookshelves while Liza wandered around, breathing in the enticing smell of a construction site.

"The floors," she murmured, admiring the quarter-cut oak.

"I haven't—" Thatcher began, only to be interrupted by Ilona's dropping a square of pale tan carpet to the floor.

"This, I thought. Then we can use a deeper shade on the walls and pick it up again in the draperies. One of my suppliers has a line of office furniture done in brushed chrome and black patent leather—costs the earth and a half, but it's marvelously effective."

Liza stared at the floor, willing her mouth to remain shut. Sacrilege, she was thinking. Gross sacrilege.

"Uh . . . that's very nice, Lonie," Thatcher mumbled. "Chrome and patent leather, huh?" The three of them stood motionless. Liza and Thatcher stared at the thick, silky square of honey-colored carpet on the raw wood floors, and Ilona's gray eyes bore into the tall man in flannel, chamois, and Harris tweed.

"I assure you, Thatch, it will be perfect. Trust me. Don't be taken in by some misguided sentimental notion just because the house is an ancient barn. The two periods go together marvelously well. In fact, anything less modern would be tacky. The contrast is what makes it work."

Liza left them to it. It was ridiculous for her to feel like crying just because she didn't agree with a professional designer about how to decorate a few office rooms that she'd probably never see again. It was none of her business if Thatcher wanted to furnish it with beanbag chairs and black-light posters. Not that there was anything cheap about the selections Ilona was putting forward. She knew enough about the cost of such things from when Corinne had insisted on redoing the whole house in Great Bridge, even though it was less than four years old when they'd bought it.

By the time the other two were ready to go, Liza had found a sunny bay window with a built-in wooden seat and curled up, seeking what little warmth she could glean through the wavery glass panes. There were no storm windows on this side of the house yet, and the panes rattled in the frames with each gust of wind. She'd been mentally remodeling the space in view, restoring a mantel that had been boxed over to make way for an oil stove and turning an enormous serving pantry into a bathroom.

"Ready to go?" Thatcher said from the doorway. "You must be freezing in here. I'm sorry we were so long, Liza. There seems to be more to this sort of thing than I had thought."

She unfolded her cramped limbs and walked stiffly over to join him. "That's all right, I enjoyed it. Houses, old or new, are fascinating to me. Always have been." Her arms were still wrapped around her, and Thatcher slipped off his tweed jacket and draped it over her shoulders. "Here, it'll swallow you, but maybe it'll help thaw you out."

She protested halfheartedly, but as the warmth from his body began to seep into her chilled bones, the perfunctory protests died on her lips. "Well, just for a minute then."

Ilona was already settled in the front seat, and she glowered when she caught sight of Liza wearing

Thatcher's coat. "If you were cold, you should have said something. The poor little match girl act went out with the bustle."

The restaurant Thatcher had selected looked like a sprawling manor house. Discreetly placed spotlights lined the circular driveway, delineating the huge oaks, and every one of the several dozen windows that showed from the front were blazing with warmth. Liza's fingers creased her corduroy skirt nervously as she wondered if it was the sort of place where a snotty maitre d' would look down his supercilious nose at her casual, inexpensive attire, but when she saw another couple, the woman wearing trousers, enter the front door, she relaxed. Besides, she was starving. Her appetite had unexpectedly deserted her at lunch today.

Thatcher had called ahead for reservations, and they were led directly to a table that looked out into the larger room from a secluded nook. He placed an order for something from the bar, selecting white wine for Liza without even bothering to consult her, and then turned his attention to the two women. "Tell me, Liza, what do you think of my new project?"

Ilona leaned forward confidingly. "If I know you, you bought the thing at rock bottom, interest and all. You could probably snap up several more the same way. White elephants like that are bound to be dirt cheap, what with energy rates rocketing, and then, when the economy levels off again, we could make a bundle on them." She raced ahead eagerly. "I have a knack with older houses. I did one recently for a gallery—rough linen walls and stark black vinyl floors—it was devastating. I kept the stained glass and all the rest of the Victorian froufrou so that the inside came as a stunning surprise." Eyes glowing with something close to warmth, her smile was clearly an invitation for a compliment, and Thatcher murmured something that sounded like, "I'll bet it did."

Liza played with the strap of her purse, and when the drinks were served, reached for hers with relief. She felt like a fifth wheel. The food would have to be out of this world to salvage much from this evening.

They had already ordered when the music began, and Ilona turned to Thatcher. "Dance with me, darling. I adore dancing with tall, tall men. It makes a girl feel so...petite, doesn't it?" She favored Liza with an insincere smile, making her feel like a giantess.

Thatcher looked from one of them to the other, instantly throwing Liza on the defensive. "Please do. I love just sitting here, soaking up the atmosphere and watching people dance, really I do!" Her cornflower eyes beseeched him not to make an issue of it. With a shrug, he turned away to lead the small blonde out to a cleared area in the middle of the room.

Liza watched them, wistful in spite of herself. Normally she didn't mind being left alone, not that it happened to her that often. It was Ilona's patronizing attitude that got under her skin. That dig about size, for instance. And if it hadn't been that, it would have been something else. The woman was a cat, that was all. Not the sort to endear herself to her own sex under any circumstances.

"Liza? Is it really you?"

Aroused from her preoccupation, Liza turned to confront Todd Hardely.

"Todd! I thought you'd be long gone," she blurted as the ruddy young man pulled out a chair and dropped into it. His crooked grin was as boyish as ever, his thick crop of bright yellow hair as disorderly.

"Back again. I hung around these parts for a few days on the off chance that you might change your mind and join me. Finally I got bored and lonesome and took off to visit the sibling in Edgewater. He's just been made commodore of his flotilla in the Coast Guard Auxiliary, and we had to celebrate that. Took me almost a week to sober up. So what about you? How come you turned down my invitation and then showed up here with Hamilton and his lady?"

Liza ignored the blatant lie. "You know Thatcher?"

"Not personally. Seen him around. He used to live in these parts, didn't he? I think Courtland knows him."

She was torn between wanting to get rid of Todd before Thatcher came back and not wanting to remain the odd one out all evening. "Are you here alone?" she asked tentatively.

"Uh...not exactly. My brother and his wife and a friend of theirs, Kathy Boone, are here with me. Kathy and Grace went to the ladies' room, and I thought I'd check out my eyesight. I couldn't believe I wasn't seeing things when you came trailing in after Hamilton and that tasty little morsel he's dancing with. Who is she, his wife?"

She didn't want to talk about Ilona. Actually, she didn't want to talk at all, and if Todd was here with his new girl friend, then the sooner he took off, the better. Aside from the fact that all these cozy twosomes weren't doing her ego much good, she didn't particularly want Todd blurting out the fact that she had been planning to spend the holiday alone with him. Nor did she want him to start wondering what she was doing here in Maryland. "As a matter of fact, I've left Barnes and Taylor. I'm working for Mr. Hamilton now. The tasty morsel happens to be an interior decorator who's doing some offices for him, and we just stopped in for a bite of dinner after working all afternoon,'' she said airily. "I didn't even have time to go home and change.''

"Hey, you look cool just the way you are, sweets. Take a word of advice. Don't try turning on the boss while that little blonde is around, or you might end up losing those gorgeous blue eyes of yours. Believe me, I cut my teeth on that type, and you're no match.''

"Thanks a bundle,'' she said dryly. It wasn't Todd's unflattering opinion that stung so, but her own knowledge that he was dead right.

He glanced over his shoulder and then grinned beguilingly at her. "Kathy's not back yet, so her loss is your gain. C'mon, let's dance. I haven't held you in my arms in too long.''

Allowing herself to be led out onto the floor, Liza diplomatically bit back an answer to that remark. She wished his Kathy luck, whoever she was. Todd had all the sincere charm of a used car salesman.

The music was uninspiring and Todd's cologne a little overpowering as he held her uncomfortably close. "Hey c'mon, bones, don't be so standoffish. Jealous 'cause I dated another girl?''

"If I'm standoffish,'' she muttered into his throat as she fought for space, "it's because lately I've got in the habit of breathing.''

She felt his mouth on her ear, and she jerked her head to one side. It amused him. From the flush on his weathered face, he was still celebrating his brother's promotion. "Todd, stop it, will you? You don't have to prove anything to me. I'll take your word for it."

Another nuzzle, and she heaved a sigh, wishing she had not let herself in for this. Todd's idea of dancing was to wrap a woman as closely as he could in a bear hug and sway on his feet while he paid her outrageous compliments. And not long ago, she'd have loved it, she thought wonderingly. At least she was being spared his blarney tonight. To think she'd once believed it—swallowed it whole and begged for more!

"Wanna chance to find out what you missed by passing up my invite?"

"Sure. Let's go over to your table, and I'll get Kathy to tell me all about it." Would the music never end?

Finally it did, and Todd led her back to her table, where, to her chagrin, she found Thatcher and Ilona seated, already starting to eat the delectable-looking seafood. Thatcher stood, his features arranged in a mask of rigid disapproval while she introduced them. She hastily took her seat and waited for Todd to remove himself, but instead he commenced a game of do-you-know with Thatcher.

THE LOVE THING 111

It seemed that Thatcher had met Courtland Hardely in the line of work, and as Todd seemed inclined to pursue the conversation to embarrassing lengths, Liza took it on herself to remind him of his obligations. "Won't Kathy be missing you?" She was uncomfortably aware of Ilona's curiosity and of Thatcher's tightly controlled displeasure, and she wondered what could have happened between him and Ilona to put him in this frigid frame of mind.

At long last Todd departed, but not without a devastating shot over his shoulder. "Give me a call, honey, and I'll come and collect you for that weekend sail you missed out on. I'm always willing to show a gal the ropes, if you know what I mean."

While her Oysters Chesapeake, with their broiled and buttered crab topping, grew cold on her plate, Liza waited for the wretched color to drain from her face. From the corner of her downcast eyes, she watched Thatcher's hands as he tore off tiny bits of roll and distributed them on the edge of his plate, but it was Ilona's speculative gaze that met hers when she finally found courage to lift her face again.

"Todd has an outrageous sense of humor," she mumbled, reaching for her wineglass. Unfortunately, her fingers struck the stem and toppled the glass, sending a flood across the damask cloth. She drew back her hand as if she'd been burned. The evening was a total disaster as far as she was concerned. The wine spill was taken care of by an attentive waiter, and she was provided with another glass. Feeling about twelve years old, she wished devoutly for it all to end. While Ilona and Thatcher carried on a calm discussion that passed completely over her head, she moved the food about her plate with a fork. She was afraid to reach for her wine again, afraid even to sip from her water glass. She'd probably choke and have to be thumped on the back if she put a bite of anything into her mouth.

"Eat your dinner, Liza," Thatcher ordered her in a hard undertone.

"Don't you start, too!" she snapped back, and at his quickly lifted eyebrows, she sagged in her chair. After all, he had done nothing to warrant her temper. For that matter, neither had anyone else, if one overlooked Todd's joking insinuation. She was simply overreacting to everything tonight, and for the life of her, she didn't know why. "I'm sorry," she mumbled, willing the time to pass so that she could escape to her own room.

On the way home some half an hour later, she leaned against the butter soft leather upholstery in the back seat and let depression wash over her in dark gray waves. She'd never been one for self-analysis, but she had to get to the root of this dreadful mood before it got out of hand. It was as if her temper was only looking for an excuse to let fly and fate perversely denied it a target, which made no sense at all!

All the same, she was acutely aware of the tension that seemed to seethe through the quiet interior of the car on the dark drive home. Ilona's displeasure was of a totally different sort from Thatcher's. Hers was like a disgruntled cat, itching to take a swipe with claws unsheathed at anyone who dared come into range, while Thatcher remained as coldly impersonal as a glacier. Liza shivered and settled deeper into her own strangely turbulent mood.

Chapter Six

The next several days were bearable only because Liza was left largely to her own devices. Ilona treated her as if she were a minor household appliance, and Thatcher, when he bothered to address her at all, spoke with such remote formality that dozens of times she asked herself why she stayed on. Each time she instinctively avoided the answer, knowing her relative peace of mind was seriously threatened. She cleaned house belligerently, cooked simple but adequate meals, and gradually learned to find her way around the small town. Thatcher gave her money for groceries, and at the end of each week he handed her a check for more than she would have earned at Barnes and Taylor in twice the time. She had argued the first time, and when he refused to take it back, stuck it behind the mirror in her bedroom, determined not to cash it.

The pups and Lady were examined, dosed, and admired by a female veterinarian who, to Liza's great relief, offered to help place them. "There's a surprising demand for mixed breed dogs these days. Too many good strains have been ruined by overbreeding. These look as if they'll be the easygoing type that make good household pets. I'd say the bitch is part Chesapeake retriever, part Airedale, and heaven knows what else. As to the paternal strain, I wouldn't even venture a guess."

Liza knew she wouldn't be able to part with the runt. An unprepossessing animal at best, the small thing had become an outlet for all Liza's pent up store of affection, a surrogate for something she desperately wanted and could never have. It was a heady sensation, having another creature so dependent on her. Lady's uncritical devotion generated a like response, and the pup's very helplessness made Liza his slave.

With the medical bill paid, she was still twelve dollars to the good. She hated having to feed her pets from Thatcher's household fund, but for the time being, it couldn't be helped. He also bought the gas for her car, since most of her driving was directly related to her housekeeping chores.

On a day when the wind blew cold and damp from the northeast, stripping the trees prematurely of their colorful leaves, she took stock of her situation. "I need my head examined for staying on here," she declared to the smallest pup, whom she had named Teddy. She gave a vicious stir to the Brunswick stew she had made from the last of the ham and some leftover chicken. "The minute your brothers and sister can be put up for adoption, we're getting out of here. I don't think I can stand any more of Princess Ilona's sweet bitchiness—no slur to your mama intended."

The older woman was skilled in the subtleties of feminine warfare, never tipping her hand when Thatcher was present. Nor was there anything overt on the rare occasions when the two women found themselves alone together. Only sidelong glances, knowing little smiles that sparkled maliciously, as if the donor were aware of some hateful, shameful secret.

Liza refused to dignify her own impotent anger by bringing it out into the open. If Ilona Clark was the sort of woman who appealed to Thatcher, then she herself could never in a million years hope to impress him.

The thought of the two of them working together all day, disappearing after dinner to listen to his favorite music in the study while Thatcher sorted through more of his father's papers, all made Liza's blood boil, and she tried desperately to root out the vicious jealousy that assailed her. She excused herself from the table each night to clear away the meal and lingered in the kitchen as long as she could. Then there were the dogs to tend and, after that, some program she declared she couldn't miss.

All in all, she wasted more time on inane television shows and unnecessary scouring than she could afford.

"Two more weeks, Teddy. Dr. Mackey said your brothers and sister could make it in a pinch, although she wouldn't recommend it. I'm afraid the pinch has come, though. The very next time I see that saccharine smile and hear that finishing school drawl asking when my little friend Todd is going to take me sailing, I'm handing in my resignation!"

Ilona had mentioned a baby brother about Liza's age several times, getting only a grunt of response from Thatcher. Her tactics were lamentably clear to anyone with eyes to see. While she stopped short of revealing her animosity in Thatcher's presence, she managed to stress both Liza's barely-out-of-the-teens status and her menial capacity in the Hamilton household. "If she had her way, I'd be out of here yesterday," Liza growled, forgetting her own determination to leave as quickly as possible.

However, she hadn't counted on Thatcher's reaction. A week later, as they were in the study having coffee and listening to the local news, she mentioned that the veterinarian had offered to help her find homes for the dogs when she got ready to leave.

"Your own dog?" he exploded. "That mangy, flea-bitten cur that I took in and bathed and fed just because it meant so damned much to you? You're giving her away?" His mouth twisted cruelly. "Your loyalty and concern overwhelm me, although just why I expected anything more from you, I couldn't say!"

Slamming down her cup, she flared back at him. "You have no right to expect anything at all of me! You don't know the first thing about me, in spite of your half-baked notion of being responsible for your cousin's stepdaughter!" They were alone for once. Ilona had kept a late appointment with her hairdresser. "You're two of a kind, you and Corinne! Hard and cold and totally unfeeling! Why I ever thought I—" She stopped the furious spate of words before she incriminated herself, leaping to her feet and turning away in an effort to contain her boiling anger. A tiny voice nagged that she was being grossly unfair; she pushed it ruthlessly away. She was already too aware of the reason for her overreaction. Never before had anyone's good opinion of her mattered so much, and for reasons that completely escaped her, Thatcher's opinion, never very high, daily sank to new depths. Her nerves were already abraded by the tension of living in an atmosphere where he and Ilona went off together each day to return only in time for dinner, laughing and discussing things of which she had no knowledge.

"I never intended—" she began, but he didn't allow her to finish telling him she had never intended getting rid of Lady—not that she knew how she could afford to feed her.

"Hard and cold and unfeeling, am I? Maybe I ought to show you just how damned hard and cold and unfeeling I really am! Obviously it takes something besides common decency to appeal to someone like you." Ignoring her outraged gasp, he caught her arms and slammed her up against the solid wall of his body, cutting off her protest with an insulting kiss. His fingers bit into her flesh, pressing harder with every feeble attempt she made to escape, and only when the small mewing sounds of her outrage registered on his consciousness did his grip begin to ease. Even then he held her immobile, one hand gripping her hair at the back of her head as his hard lips moved relentlessly over her mouth, her eyes, the hollows beneath her cheeks. She could feel the heavy pounding of his heartbeat through the thin wool of her sweater, and his breath was a ragged sound in her ears, a hot current on her sensitive skin. One of her arms had been trapped between them, and she discovered her fingers were curling and uncurling on his hip. She froze, stunned at her own growing need.

Somehow, without her being aware of his having moved, she found herself pressed between the back cushions of the sofa and Thatcher's hard body. He was kissing her again, slowly, expertly now, robbing her of every remnant of self-respect as she felt herself catch fire from the driving force of his own arousal.

Twisting her head away, she felt his mouth seek out the hollows of her ear. She shuddered and whispered a weak protest. "Thatcher, please...please." He held her still with one thigh across her own, and as he moved her against him slowly, deliberately, with one hand, his other hand sought the small rise of her breast, teasing the already engorged nipples into hardened peaks of tingling sensation.

"Is this what you want, Liza? Is this what you need from a man? Is this what you came all this way to get from that half-grown specimen you were draped around the other night?" The hot, firm flesh of his lips moved against her throat with every word, driving her into a frenzy.

"No, no, no," she sighed, but he ignored her feeble efforts at denial. They both knew she was lying, at least as far as her present needs were concerned.

She could no more refuse him now than she could fly to the moon.

"Why did you run out on him, Liza? Didn't he offer you enough? What made you run out on him at the last minute?" His fingers were tracing patterns on the silken skin just above the waistband of her jeans; they paused at the top button.

"Stop it, Thatcher," she groaned, almost out of her mind with the compelling needs of her own body. She had never experienced anything like it before. It was as if she were being dragged down into a sea of quicksand, longing not for rescue, but to be allowed to drown herself completely.

"Were you as maddeningly wanton with him as you are with me? Did you drive him out of his mind with that innocent face, that deceptively childish body of yours?"

His words aroused some small, still functioning part of her brain, and she realized she was caressing him with all the unschooled eagerness at her command. Her hands were playing about his lean, hard waist, making daring little excursions under the loose tail of his chamois shirt. "Thatcher, don't spoil it by saying ugly things," she pleaded, willing her hungry hands to momentary stillness.

Dimly, she sensed some alien force in him, some part of him that stood aside from the all too evident needs of his body. It was as if he had a powerful need to hurt her at the same time he was making love to her, to drive in on her the cruel knowledge that he despised her even as she was giving in to him. Bewildered, she began to protest, but he cut off her words.

His tongue traced the line between her swollen lips, and then he leaned away and stared into her soft-focused eyes. "Tell me, how long have you known young Hardely? Was he the one? He must have been pretty damned young at the time. You couldn't have known what you were doing, but he damned well did, so what did he offer you...money? Was that the attraction? Because if it was, then you might say I'm collecting now on a long overdue debt."

Long afterwards, Liza thought she must have imagined the raw pain she sensed in his voice as he ground out those searing words. She had only time to demand of him what he meant, to hear a fragment of his grim reply, when the sound of Ilona's car outside startled them both into hasty action.

"What...what are you getting at?" she whispered in agonized disbelief.

"The money you needed all those years ago? The money you thought came from Corinne?" His eyes were in shadow. She stared at the thin, implacable line of his mouth. It still held the sheen of her kisses.

"The...the money? You mean that was yours?"

"My cousin and I might not have much in common, but when she's in need, family ties count for a lot. Only that time, it was your need, wasn't it?"

Liza could only nod. In her bewilderment, there was no room for reason, no time to root out the source of the contempt that lurked just under the surface of the compelling physical attraction between them. At the sound of Ilona's entry, Thatcher levered himself up, tucking his shirttail back into his lean trousers. Distraught, Liza made her escape through the other door of the study and up the back staircase. Ilona's husky drawl followed her as she raced recklessly up the dark, narrow steps.

"Hello, darling. Sorry to be so late. I know how you hate being stuck with that poor, awkward girl of Corinne's."

God! *He* had supported her all those years ago! The monthly checks that had come from the lawyer, the money she had thought Corinne deposited for her—money that had had to stretch impossibly thin to cover rent, her skimpy meals, the school fees, and what few clothes she absolutely had to have—it had been his! In a hurt, blind rage, she pushed the mirror to one side and snatched the two checks she had hidden behind it, tearing them into bits and watching with bitter satisfaction as the pale blue confetti drifted to the floor.

But then, what had happened to the small portion of the estate that was supposed to come to her? she wondered as the heat of her rage abated. Her father wouldn't have given Rosalyn's things to his new bride. Corinne had said everything had to go to satisfy the creditors, and Liza had been too numb to question her. She had sat like a bump on a log while the lawyer had gone over the details of the estate with them, her mind drifting somewhere in limbo as they discussed things a child of just under fifteen found totally incomprehensible. Corinne had jerked at her elbow impatiently at the end of the interview. "Come on then, Liza. There's nothing else to be gained here. It's a total washout!"

The numbness of grief had still enveloped her when Corinne had told her that she had a chance of a good job out west and that there was no point in bothering with social workers and foster homes for the short time left before Liza came of age. "Just stay out of trouble, Liza. Keep a low profile, and no one will ever question you. You sure as hell won't miss me, and I can do without a beanstalk of a girl poking along after me like a lost dog. I'll see that you have enough in the bank to cover your expenses, so there's no reason for us to have to bother with the authorities or each other from now on. What they don't know can't hurt us."

The law said she had to stay in school until she was sixteen. She managed to stay on and graduate at nearly seventeen. By then the money had long since stopped coming. At that point Liza had a regular list of babysitting clients anyway, and made good money on her own, with time to study after she had bedded down her charges. During the summer she worked in a day nursery, a job she got through the recommendation of one of her clients.

Staring blindly at the delicate pattern on the French wallpaper, she wondered now why on earth a perfect stranger would have paid to support her all those years ago. A niece, perhaps, or even a cousin's child, but a cousin's stepdaughter? It just didn't make sense. No one was that generous, that altruistic, especially when most of the time they gave every evidence of cold disapproval.

But not all of the time, a voice whispered mockingly.

Torn between a desperate need to leave so as to put the whole untenable situation behind her and a growing feeling of indebtedness, she paced restlessly in the large bedroom until she felt as if she'd explode. Downstairs, Thatcher and Ilona would be cozily ensconced in the study. She had no doubt they were lovers, although she'd never seen any evidence of it. No doubt their long hours spent in the office weren't altogether wasted.

Ilona had made sure Liza knew that the Hamiltons and the Clarks had been a part of the same social set practically since the *Mayflower*. The Clarks owned a vacation condominium at Jupiter Beach in Florida, while the Hamiltons had always lived here on the Eastern Shore. They had traded off on occasion until over the years the families had drifted apart.

It was quite obvious to Liza, if not to Thatcher, that Ilona had every intention of stopping that drift. The blonde was far too experienced to tip her hand prematurely, but Liza's instincts, honed to a fine edge by her own vulnerability where Thatcher was concerned, unerringly picked up each small clue. Ilona might have set her sights, but the final shot wasn't fired yet.

A less shrewd woman might have ousted Liza after the first day. Ilona was smarter than that. More than once she had mentioned Thatcher's unfortunate penchant for collecting strays and his overgrown sense of responsibility. "Which makes me something between a poor relation and another Lady," Liza muttered as she stared down through the naked trees at the cold glitter of moonlight on the river.

Oh, Lord, what am I doing here? I'm twenty years old, and I've been supporting myself for years! I have a car. Nobody's handcuffed me to the bedstead. So why don't I walk out that door and keep going? She expelled an exasperated sigh and rejected the answer. Emotions were no good to her now. For once, she was going to have to use a little cool, calm deliberation and come up with the proper answer. None of this dashing off on a wild goose chase or leading with her head and her knee while she walked into the side of a moving vehicle. Think first, then act.

She had already allowed herself to be provoked into making her first mistake. Balefully, she glared down at the litter on the floor. She'd worked hard for that money, even though it was far too much. Still, if that was the going rate for cook-housekeepers in this part of the country, who was she to complain?

But it wasn't. Not when her employer—she refused to think of him as anything more—not when he threw in room and board, driving expenses, and pet care. Not to mention the occasional light lovemaking, she thought with a deliberate twist of the knife. Still, her own funds wouldn't get her very far. If she chose to drive back the way she had come, she'd use more gas. If she went south on Route 50 down the Eastern Shore, there was the Bay Tunnel toll, which was almost more than the sum total of her funds.

So much for melodramatic gestures. She'd have to take it from the housekeeping money and repay it as soon as she landed another job. Having spent sixty-seven dollars and forty-three cents on groceries for three people and half a dozen dogs just yesterday, it would be a few days before she could expect any more. She'd just have to be patient and bide her time. This time she wouldn't make the mistake of announcing her intentions in advance. She'd drop off the dogs on her way, leaving a note behind. Thatcher knew her address in Chesapeake, of course, but he wouldn't be inclined to pursue her that far. Not even his misplaced sense of responsibility stretched to that extent.

And if it did, she reminded herself, if he were inclined to call just to be sure she arrived safely, he'd have Ilona beside him to see that his interest didn't get out of bounds again.

She slept finally. By closing her mind to the ache inside her, she managed to get several hours of dreamless sleep, from which she awakened feeling utterly leaden.

As usual, she served breakfast for Thatcher and Ilona in the small, sunny breakfast room and waited until they had left to fix her own. She had fallen into the habit of having cheese and butter on brown bread along with a mug of strong, freshly brewed coffee. She ate it curled up on the sofa under an afghan while she leafed through the morning papers.

Thatcher took three dailies and a couple of weeklies. In one of them there was a home buyers' and builders' section sponsored by the local realtors' association. She pored over it, studying plans, criticizing, mentally revising, meanwhile sprinkling it liberally with crumbs that would later have to be vacuumed up.

She no longer really wanted to tackle the extensive program required to get a degree in architecture. She knew her own shortcomings all too well by now, and even if she had the money, she doubted that she'd have the patience. She had taken mechanical drawing in high school and had improved her skills at home by dint of practice. If she could just get a job with a building contractor, with anyone connected with the building trade, she might gradually be able to work her way into having a voice in the planning, just to be around new lumber, to inhale the resinous scent of pine and fir, the exotic fragrance of cedar and juniper.

"And that's another thing, damn his hide!" she growled, as she recalled Thatcher's having mentioned being up to his knees in wood shavings that first day she had spent here. He'd been busy remodeling his offices even then and her own stiff-necked pride had not allowed her to get involved. He probably thought she wouldn't be interested—if he thought about her at all.

She was running the vacuum when she thought she heard the phone. Switching off the noisy machine, she listened. It was the door buzzer. Dropping the contraption where it was, she hurried to see who on earth would be calling at eleven o'clock in the morning.

"Yes?" she greeted cautiously, the chain still fastened on the wide front door. There was nothing threatening about the attractive young man who stood rocking back on the heels of his Bean mocs, hands shoved in the pockets of his corduroy jeans.

"Hi, Liza Calahan. Could I interest you in a set of encyclopedias, or maybe a ninety-seven-piece set of genuine plastic cookware, guaranteed for a lifetime of joyful indigestion?"

Her wide mouth twisted into a grin despite herself. "If you can prove your name's not Clark, I'll buy two sets of everything." There was no mistaking the honey blond hair that fell just short of being reddish. She had thought Ilona's came from a bottle, but evidently it was a family trait, as were the long, rather narrow gray eyes. But in this case, the eyes were warm, quizzical, and definitely approving. "You're Ilona's brother, Jeffrey."

"Actually, it's Jefferson," he admitted modestly, and Liza groaned as she unfastened the chain and opened the door wider.

"It would be."

Jeff reached behind him and picked up a soft leather bag. "Yeah, it do be a bit much. The middle name's Gilbert, too, and Mum swears she's a direct descendant of Sir Walter Raleigh's half brother, although it's a historical fact that the poor devil never married."

"If we're getting into genealogy, would you care to hear my grandfather's tales of how he avoided the potato famine by taking a cruise? Steerage, of course."

"But of course! Only the grossly insecure would put up with the boredom of going first class," said Jeff Clark.

Liza liked him immediately in spite of the fact that he reminded her of Todd Hardely—the same carefully ratty uniform, the same air of healthy, good-natured arrogance. She could have sworn they both had the same dentist, judging by the uniformity and perfection of their broad, uncomplicated grins. Suddenly, for no reason she could fathom, she felt a hundred years old. "Your sister's not here at the moment. She's been helping Thatcher with his new offices in Easton."

"Yeah, that's what she said when she invited me to hop down for a spell. Something about you being all alone with no one to call your own, la de dah."

Liza looked curiously over her shoulder as she led the way back to the study. "Excuse the machinery. I was cleaning up after my breakfast."

Jeff dropped his carryall and, brushing aside a stack of newspapers, sprawled in one of the wing chairs. "Yeah, sure, we all clean up after a meal with the vac. Do it all the time myself. So what else do you do around these parts, Liza Calahan?"

Jeff helped himself to one of Thatcher's cigars from the humidor on the table as they chatted about the area, with which Liza was barely familiar, and about an upcoming regatta of which she knew nothing at all. Then Jeff flashed his flawless teeth again and told her she must have done something to get old Lonie in a swivel.

"I don't know about you, but I'm really here as a double agent, you know. A sort of red herring to draw you off Thatch's trail. Lonie's afraid he'll slip away from her greedy little clutches again, I guess."

"Twaddle! If you really want to know, I'm here because your friend Thatcher has an overdeveloped social conscience and his cousin Corinne walked out on her job of stepmother after my father died. For some reason, Thatcher feels responsible." She shrugged slender shoulders. It was really none of his business, of course, but at this point she was beyond caring. If Ilona knew about his paying her expenses her last two years in school—and, of course, she did—then probably she had told her kid brother. "I guess he sort of won me by default." She grinned halfheartedly.

"Whatever," Jeff dismissed breezily. "Anyway, Lonie invited me, and I can afford to cut a few classes, since I'm flunking out, anyway. Besides, I'd just as soon be out of reach when my dad finds out."

Liza fixed sandwiches for them both. Jeff helped himself to a beer, disdaining the use of a glass. He admired the pups, told her about his own Labradors, and then invited her to go down to the marina to see who was in port.

Of course, Todd would be long gone by now, not that it would bother her to run into him again, but Liza begged off on the pretext of having to start dinner. She watched Jeff drive off in an open car that she dimly recognized as British, then considered how she could use him to help her get away. If that made her mercenary, then so be it. Meanwhile, she supposed she'd have to put him in the one remaining bedroom. Thatcher, of course, had the first-floor suite his parents used when they were here. She rather thought he'd been using one of the second-floor rooms until she came, when he'd tactfully switched. That left her in the blue room, Ilona in the master bedroom, and now Jeff in the spare.

Chummy. Not that she was worried. Jeff was about as threatening to her as Teddy. In fact, there was something of the overgrown puppy about both Jeff and Todd, come to think of it, although Todd was several years older. Neither one of them would be flattered by the comparison, though, she acknowledged wryly. Odd how she'd aged so in a few short days. If Thatcher was overly conscious of the dozen or so years between them, then that was his problem. Age only added to the potency of his masculine appeal where she was concerned. But then, her comparative youth was not the only thing he held against her. Somewhere he'd gained the impression that she was not only fast, but unreliable as well. And mercenary? Did he think she had known about the money he'd given her? It hadn't occurred to her at the time that she wasn't entitled to something from her father's estate—surely there had been an insurance policy of some sort.

Admittedly, she hadn't gone into it very deeply. Family finances had never concerned her, and after her father's unexpected death, money had been the last thing on her mind.

But mercenary? Couldn't he understand that she hadn't asked anything of anyone at the time, accepting whatever arrangements Corinne had made without question? If she had wanted anything—anything material, that was—it would have been her mother's collection of cranberry glass, not that it had been particularly valuable. Just lovely and reminiscent of the quiet, gentle woman whose memory grew dimmer and dimmer with each passing year.

And on the painful subject of Thatcher Hamilton, what had Jeff meant when he'd said his sister was afraid he'd slip through her fingers . . . again?

Chapter Seven

In spite of her apprehensiveness, dinner was almost enjoyable. There was no sign of the tension she had dreaded, and afterwards the four of them sipped Irish coffee in the study. Jeff carried the conversational ball, asking Thatcher all sorts of questions about what had happened to so-and-so, people he remembered from when he'd visited the Hamiltons several years ago. They argued the merits of wooden versus fiberglass hulls, which led to a discussion of the Chesapeake oystering fleet, which operated for the most part under sail.

"I don't think Liza's had a chance to do much sightseeing, Jeff," his sister drawled in her deep, husky tones. "Why don't you show her around while you're here. Thatch and I can manage on our own for a few days, and it would be a shame for her to have to go back home without seeing anything. I doubt if the poor girl has had a real day off since she's been here.''

So I'm on my way home, Liza mused, wondering if the tightening of Thatcher's jaw had been a mere trick of the lighting. Perhaps he didn't care for the implication that he mistreated his domestic help. He'd grown almost broodingly quiet, leaning back in his chair to stare into the depths of the dark liquid in his tall, thin cup.

It stormed sometime after midnight, a freak autumn thunderstorm. Liza sat bolt upright in bed, wondering what had awakened her. Slowly she became aware of the rumble of distant thunder. With each clap came an eerie wail from somewhere outside her open window.

Lady. They had moved the dogs from the basement to an old, unused shed just yesterday, and she realized they shared her feelings about thunderstorms. Just as relief flooded through her at determining the source of the unearthly wailing, a stunning clap of thunder almost lifted her from her bed. She shrieked and covered her ears. Oh, Lord, this was no time to crawl under the bed and cringe.

That hound would arouse the dead, at the rate she was going.

Tossing on the faded navy blue flannel robe she'd worn since high school days, she collected her shoes and made her way barefoot down the stairs. The rain seemed to have stopped, at least. Carol had mailed her a care package, but had forgotten to include her raincoat and boots. Leaving the back door unlatched, Liza had just braced herself for the dash across the dark, wet back yard when Jeff spoke from behind her.

"What's happening? Hound of the Baskervilles on the loose?" He joined her in the doorway, draping an arm across her shoulders. "If that god-awful noise came from your mutt, I'm glad you put her outside."

"You don't happen to have a flashlight on you, do you?" Liza asked. She remembered seeing one somewhere around the house, but she hadn't the faintest idea where.

"Let's go out the front way and stop by my car. I've got one there." He led the way and Liza followed, grateful for his company. The dog had calmed down now that the worst of the storm seemed to have passed, but she could hear the pups crying. She didn't want to risk Lady's getting restless and running out on them. Considering her nomadic background, that was a distinct possibility.

"Hell," Jeff complained. The bottom dropped out just as they reached his rakish sports car. "Come on, get in. It'll blow over in a minute or two, this is just the postlude. Moon's already beginning to show through those clouds over there." He held the door for her and then ran around the driver's side to escape the sudden flurry of rain.

"Cozy," he murmured, stretching his arm across the back of her bucket seat. "Smoke?"

"No thanks." She watched the sky warily, wishing she had made a dash for the shed instead of the car. Still, without the flashlight she wouldn't have been able to see a thing. They sat there for perhaps five minutes, and then Jeff leaned across her lap to fumble in the glove compartment for the flashlight. He found it, but the batteries were dead.

"Sorry 'bout that, Liza. Dogs sound okay now anyhow, so why don't we go in and scrounge something to eat?"

"I'd better look in on them, just in case," she insisted. "Maybe the sound of my voice will do the trick, even though they can't see me." She didn't actually relish the idea of blundering around in a shed full of discarded gardening tools. Considering her past track record, she'd probably trip over a bag of fertilizer and break her leg.

"Meet you in the kitchen then," Jeff promised, but she grabbed his hand and pulled him along behind her.

"Oh, no you don't. If I'm going barging around here in the dark, I'm not going alone, you can bet on it!" She laughed, charged into a prickly wet japonica, swore, and then swore again as she blundered onto the soft ground of the iris bed.

By the time she made it back to the house, with Jeff one step behind her, she was soaked through. Her ankles had been thoroughly licked clean by half a dozen eager tongues, but the gown she wore under her disreputable woolen robe was bound to be ruined. She could picture the crystal-sharp accordion pleats smeared with mud and liberally laced with an assortment of twigs, briars, and Lord knows what else. If Carol weren't such a scatterbrain, she would have sent along a pair of pajamas—preferably the cotton flannel ones with the feet in them.

"Gad, I'm drenched! Greater love hath no man and all that rot. Come on, woman, make me a sandwich and a cup of cocoa, will you?" Jeff wore a trenchcoat over his pajamas. When he peeled it off and tossed it onto a kitchen chair, it didn't occur to Liza to be embarrassed. Jefferson Clark could have been a brother, or even a sister, for all the sexual feeling he aroused in her, which was really rather odd. He was certainly good-looking, in a clean-cut, boyish sort of way. Somehow, you knew his mother had taken all the proper vitamins when she was carrying him, and she had probably played tennis into her seventh month.

She heated milk for cocoa while Jeff removed half the contents of the refrigerator, arranging them on the table and standing back to survey the lineup thoughtfully. They were discussing the merits of jelly versus mayonnaise with peanut butter when the milk boiled over. They both dashed for the stove, colliding in the process. Liza managed to slide the pan off the burner. Jeff was still hanging onto her when Thatcher spoke from the doorway.

"What the hell is going on here, would you mind telling me?" He glared at first one, then the other, and Liza found herself staring back at him, her breath caught somewhere at the back of her throat. Unlike her, he had not stopped to put on a robe. The tobacco brown pajama pants he wore were his only garment, and it occurred to her to wonder if he wore even that much in the summertime. She found her eyes caught in the tangle of dark body hair that curled on his chest and arrowed downward. Somehow he had managed to get the sort of tan that lasted year-round, and there was no line of demarcation where the pants rode low on his lean hips.

The tableau broke up and shifted. Jeff rounded up an armload of sandwich ingredients to replace them in the refrigerator. "I think cocoa and a hunk of cheese will do me," he mumbled. Liza turned to wipe up the milky mess off the top of the range.

"Leave it," Thatcher snarled.

"It'll stick."

"Leave it! Unless you shut the shed door, that dog of yours is going to take off before the night's over... and good riddance."

"You'd like that, wouldn't you? It would suit you just fine if we all took off. Well, maybe you'll get lucky! I couldn't budge the blasted thing. I think the hinges are rusted stiff. And anyway, the storm's over now." Right now she wanted only to escape the burning scrutiny of his metallic eyes. They were like brass, hard, hot brass. "You're certainly in a lovely mood," she accused sullenly.

"I don't take kindly to being awakened in the middle of the night." Unnoticed by either of them Jeff had taken his snack and disappeared from the room.

"Oh, I'm so sorry," Liza said with exaggerated courtesy. "Next time I plan a thunderstorm, I'll try to pick a more convenient hour."

"Watch it, Liza." Thatcher held the back door open, a flashlight in his other hand. "Come on."

"I don't see why you need me to go with you," she protested, taking care to avoid touching him as she edged past him onto the gleaming wetness of the brick patio. This whole expedition was totally unnecessary. If Lady had been going to escape, she'd be gone by now. "They're all right, I tell you. Jeff and I checked them not ten minutes ago."

"Did you? Or did you just use that as a handy excuse to meet after you thought everyone else would be asleep?" He was stalking along behind her, practically treading on her heels, and she had to hold herself back to keep from breaking into a run. "I heard both doors of his car, you know."

She stopped and spun around, almost colliding with him. "You're unbelievable! Just what sort of person do you think I am, anyway?"

"I don't think you really want me to go into that, do you?" He took her by the arm, practically dragging her the few yards to the old gardening shed. Flashing the light inside, he stood in the doorway, and Liza watched in helpless anger as he played the light over the squirming mass of fur that surrounded the mongrel bitch. Lady stared back at them calmly, her nerves and her family all nicely settled down for the night. "I'll close up, anyway," Thatcher muttered, lifting the heavy, sagging door and swinging it over the clumps of grass. "We can let her out again first thing in the morning."

Liza had the strange impression that the door and the dogs were the least of his worries. For all the snarling anger in his voice, he seemed somehow distracted. She followed him back across the wet lawn. Just as he reached the brick patio, he snapped off the light and placed it on a wrought-iron table.

Turning to face her, he said, "Liza." Just that, her name. She waited, hardly breathing, for what was to come next. "Jeff's in enough trouble at home without your adding to it. Go easy on him, will you? The last thing he needs now is to get mixed up with someone like you. In fact, I think Ilona made a big mistake in asking him here."

Someone like her! What was that supposed to mean? Rage rose up like a red tide and swept away all reason. Without thinking, she raised a hand and swung it full force against the side of his face. Her palm burned. It sounded like a shot and it burned like the very devil. She began to yell. "I hate you! I...I..." She could think of no words to describe the agonizing mixture of feelings that choked her, and tears of rage sprang to her eyes. She lifted a fist to pound on his chest, but he caught it and twisted it behind her back, arching her against his body. Even in the chill of the late October sky, his body was warm, burning against her damp skin in the few places not covered by her bathrobe.

"Oh, no you don't, you little hellcat! It doesn't take much to make you revert to type, does it? A little overdue plain talking and you turn into a street urchin! No wonder Corinne—"

"To hell with Corinne! To hell with you and your whole blasted family! I don't need you, Thatcher Hamilton. I don't want your rotten charity or your...your snooty friends. I'll pay back every damned cent you ever spent on me if I have to rob a bank to do it!"

"There are easier ways for your sort," he sneered, crushing the delicate bones of her wrist as he jerked her arm even higher behind her back.

"Ouch! Damn it, if you want to play rough, I can play that game, too." She kicked out and connected solidly with his shin. She was wearing her hard leather-soled flats. Thatcher released her wrist and doubled over. Unfortunately, his head struck hers and they both staggered back.

Thatcher gave vent to a low-voiced stream of profanity as Liza recovered enough to edge away from him. By this time she was hurting all over. Some deep-seated shred of wisdom told her that although her head and her arm might recover, there were deeper wounds that would leave scars for as long as she lived. By now, her anger had disintegrated into a desperate need to get away, and she glanced wildly around her. Her eyes lighted on her car, pulled up close beside the three-car garage where Thatcher's and Ilona's cars were kept along with the elder Hamilton's Seville.

Moving with the jungle poise of a big cat, Thatcher shifted so that he was between her and the cars. "Oh, no you don't," he growled.

"You can't stop me!" She could lock herself in her car and freeze to death, she thought, wiping her eyes with the back of her hand. Without her keys, she wouldn't get very far, but at least she'd be safe for the moment. Oh, Lord, how did she get herself into such impossible situations? And why did he despise her so? Surely what she'd done all those years ago hadn't been that reprehensible, even though it wasn't strictly legal. His precious cousin had arranged it, after all.

Heaving a sigh, she suddenly realized she was behaving irrationally. She was soaking wet. Her arm ached and her head ached and, worst of all, her heart ached—not to mention her stupid pride. "I give up," she said tiredly. "I'll do whatever you want me to do. Only please, Thatcher, *please* just let me go home." Shivering suddenly as a damp gust blew a flurry of wet leaves down on them, she awaited his verdict. Whatever he held against her, this was no time to go into it. If she didn't catch pneumonia, he would. He wore rubber moccasins with no socks. Those, along with the silky pajama pants, were all he had on, and the temperature must be down in the forties. "You know," she observed with weary detachment, "you're insane."

He nodded slowly, opening the screened door to allow her to go inside. "You noticed. Well, if it's any comfort to you, I agree with you. I'm doing my level best to fight it, but times like these don't help matters much. Here, get out of that wet rag and let me dry you off," he ordered, pulling a towel from the kitchen rack. His hands were on the shoulders of her robe. She clutched it tightly around her. "What's the matter, don't you trust me?" he said, with a bitter smile. "Then you're wiser than I gave you credit for being." His eyes moved over her with a fevered sort of intensity, and Liza fought against an irrational urge to lean against him. Instead, she edged away, only to find herself up against the table.

He followed her, standing so close his legs brushed against the damp length of her bathrobe. With hopeless resignation, Liza watched the flicker of emotion cross his face before it tightened into its usual enigmatic planes. "Don't try to stop me now, Liza. God knows, I get little enough sleep as it is, thinking about you up there in the room over my head. Tonight... Tonight it'll be impossible."

His voice was dark brown velvet, shaded with a tired sort of desperation. It drew her with an irresistible magnetism, and she found herself unable to move away when he reached for her. His hands came down on her shoulders gently this time, rounding, cupping the delicate bones, slipping under the heavy cloth of her robe to stroke her warm skin. "Liza, Liza, why did you have to come back into my life? You were a dream, just an impossible, embarrassing dream I had managed to put out of my conscious mind, and then you rose up in front of me like some Irish-eyed Nemesis, my own Daughter of the Night." He laughed harshly. "God! Is that ever apt."

"I don't know what you're talking about," she whispered, the strain in her voice rendering it barely audible. Her nerves were trembling like threads of finely spun glass, attenuated long past the breaking point.

"I know you don't, Liza. You couldn't possibly know the sort of hell an otherwise rational man can build for himself." The stroking hands had slipped the robe from her shoulders now, and when she tore her eyes away from the agonized fire in his and turned half away from him, he twisted her so that she was leaning back against the cool surface of his naked chest. "I want you so much, and it's driving me crazy... *crazy!*" He was fingering the lace straps of her nightgown while his mouth moved up and down the shallow valley of her nape, and she could feel the quiet thunder of his heart against her back.

It was crazy, all right. It was dangerously, wonderfully insane. It was against everything she had ever taught herself—the hard-won common sense, the instinct for self-preservation—but she was helpless against his particular brand of insanity. Why couldn't she have developed some early warning system to save her from this trap, to warn her of the flaw in her defenses? The tiny crack in the dam that held back the tide of her feelings widened slowly, inexorably, until there was no holding back the flood waters. She was going to drown. Turning blindly in his strong arms, she reached for her fate with closed eyes and parted lips.

There was no warning. The sudden tearing sound of harshly indrawn breath was the first indication Liza had that they were not alone. She opened her eyes, and it was as if she had been in a dark room for a long, long time and then someone had suddenly turned on a bright light. Ilona stood in the doorway, her face unnaturally white in the fluorescent gleam.

To his credit—or possibly not—Thatcher did not release her immediately. Instead of guiltily pushing her from him, he held her there for the few moments it took to gain control of his voice. And then with a calmness at which Liza could only marvel, he asked, "Did you want something, Ilona?"

Liza stood in the center of her bedroom, staring in the mirror at the specter of her own white face. Her hair was on end, its healthy sheen belying the bruised-looking shadows under her enormous cloudy blue eyes. The familiar bathrobe was a ludicrous accompaniment to the seductive gown underneath, the gown that had been clearly in evidence when Ilona had made her untimely appearance.

Untimely! God, it was the most timely interruption that could have happened. One more minute and Thatcher would have swung her up into his arms and carried her to his bed, and from there on, she would have been lost. Nothing in her lifetime had prepared her for the realization that heaven and hell were separated by only a heartbeat of time. Heaven for the brief moment when her own surrender could blind her to the fact that he despised her, even while he was physically attracted to her. Hell forever afterward as she tried to forget.

Oh, she'd seen the love-hate thing growing in him. She was wise enough to recognize that he was fighting something in his own nature, something that permitted him to give in to the demands of his body but forbade any real relationship between them. He'd shut her out of almost every phase of his existence, deliberately using Ilona as a buffer.

Good Lord, did he think she was fooled by his talk of protecting her reputation? As far as he was concerned, she had none. From the lofty height of his irreproachable background, he looked down on a little Irish nobody who had been on her own since she was fourteen and a half, obviously considering her no more than a street waif, an object of his own charity. That same insufferable streak of misguided idealism that had made him offer to support her until she was old enough to leave school had done him in again. Of all the people in the world she had chosen to throw herself at that night when Todd had let her down, why did it have to be him?

Somewhere in the distance she heard the phone ring once, and then it was silent. Who would be calling in the middle of the night? And then she blinked and looked at her watch. It was almost tomorrow—today, that is. In a little while the sun would be glistening on the red oak and the wine-colored sweet gum leaves, turning the yellow maples and sycamores into incandescent balls of light. The bay would be that deep, almost purplish gray, and hundreds of weekend sailors would unfurl their Dacron sails long after the skipjacks and bugeyes had gone out under heavy canvas to the oyster beds.

And Liza Calahan would be leaving it all behind, closing her eyes to the unexpected beauty she had found, her mind to the unbearable ache inside her.

Shaking off the veil of self-pity, she dropped her robe and gown on the floor and crossed to the bathroom. From Jeff's room beyond came the sound of snoring, and she grinned reluctantly. So much for his designs on her—or his sister's designs on his behalf. She supposed she should feel flattered that Ilona had felt threatened enough to call in reinforcements, but somehow it had ceased to matter. For all she cared, someone could stuff all the Hamiltons and the Hardelys and the Clarks into a duffel bag and drop them off the Bay Bridge. From now on she'd stick to her own sort—whatever that was. At least she wouldn't be made to feel as if her very existence were a blight on the face of the earth.

When she finally came downstairs, Jeff greeted her with the news that Thatcher had had to go to Baltimore and Ilona had gone with him. "Something came up at the office. He's got a whole regiment of legal types working for him, but I gather that between all the yachts and fishing boats confiscated for drug running and all this mess with refugees coming ashore on anything that floats, they've got half the government agencies on the back of their necks."

Wavering between relief and dismay at her unexpected reprieve, Liza accepted the cup of coffee Jeff poured for her and dropped into one of the rush-bottomed chairs. "I'm taking off myself in a few hours," she admitted. She still didn't know how far she'd get on the money she had. If only she hadn't been so darned hasty in tearing up those checks. Still, she certainly couldn't hang around here any longer. Her ego couldn't take it, even if her common sense would allow it.

"Hey, I don't think that's going to work out," Jeff said plaintively. "I've got my marching orders, too.

Thatch called my old man and tipped him off that I was A.W.O.L., and he came down on me with both feet. I've got to get back to school and hit the books. If I flunk out, I can look for the nearest shovel and start earning my living digging ditches.''

"So?"

"So," Jeff repeated, "Thatch is expecting you to hang around and look after things until he gets off the hook."

"That's silly! What needs looking after? I'll lock all the doors and windows, water the plants, and stop deliveries if he plans to be gone more than a day or so, but—"

"But nothing. This place got ripped off last summer when Aunt Jean and Uncle Car were out in Arizona. That's why they wouldn't go on this cruise until Thatch agreed to look after things for them."

Pulling her eyes away from Thatcher's old Shetland sweater on the back of the basement door, Liza murmured, "I didn't know you were related to the Hamiltons." Had she mistaken the relationship between Thatcher and Ilona? Surely it wasn't just cousinly interest that had brought the blonde down here at the first indication of competition.

Jeff immediately blasted any feeble hopes in that direction. "Oh, it's just a courtesy title. We grew up in and out of each other's homes, and you know how it is. I was too close to call them Mr. and Mrs. Hamilton and too young for Car and Jean. You gonna stay on? Thatch left an envelope for you on the desk in the study." He looked at her hopefully, saw the uncertainty on her face, and grinned as he pushed his chair away from the table. "If it's okay with you, I think I'll just make me a sandwich or two for the road. I'm spent out until the old man sends along my quarterly pittance."

Liza ended up making a stack of sandwiches, and she located a Thermos and filled it with juice. "If there's any more of that cake thing we had last night, I wouldn't object to finishing it off for you," Jeff said over her shoulder when he came downstairs with his carryall. He nuzzled the side of her neck through her hair. She leaned away and laughed in spite of her misery. "Hey, you know, you're a mighty fine gal," he teased. "If Lonie bumps you, why don't you hang around and wait for me to finish school? I've got a job all ready and waiting in Dad's office, and we could have a ball together."

Half amused, half touched, she asked, "Is that a proposal or a job offer?"

"You know, I'm not sure," he answered bemusedly. "I won't put anything in writing, but stick around, will you?"

She handed over his lunch. "Don't count on it," she retorted dryly, not resisting when he planted an enthusiastic if somewhat inexpert kiss on the corner of her mouth. She watched as he drove off with a gutsy roar and a wave and then, arms wrapped around her against the brisk midmorning wind, she strolled out to the shed to let Lady out for a run.

The shed door was propped open and a streak of sunlight extended into its musty interior to pick out the tangle of puppies romping over Lady's sedate form. They rushed to greet her. Liza knelt on the dry earth floor and picked up each one in turn, reaching last of all for her favorite. "Teddy, what should I do? He's gone and ruined it all now. I had built up my nerve. I was so blasted mad with him last night that I didn't care if I never saw him again, but if I stay, it'll start all over again. And if I don't, that will be the end of everything, and I'm not sure I can stand it."

She wandered into the kitchen and put the breakfast things in to soak while she mixed the dogs' cereal. She had been weaning them in order to turn them over to Dr. Mackey, and the job was almost done. They were growing visibly, and soon she'd be hard put to afford their keep. There was also another trip to the vet for permanent shots and things of that sort coming up, and she'd just as soon share the burden.

Not until the chores were done and the dogs moved out into a temporary fenced area to play did she go into the study. For long moments she stared at the envelope bearing her name on the desk. She was fascinated by Thatcher's handwriting, unconsciously comparing it with what she knew of the man himself.

Her name was boldly inscribed in black ink, the slanting letters tall and well formed. There was a gracefulness about the capital *L* and the loop of the *z* that intrigued her, and she wished her name were much longer. She wished she had a book on graphology. She wished she knew what there was about Thatcher Hamilton that made her love him so desperately against all reason, all common sense. Lord knows, he had done everything to discourage that love, but it had been like trying to root out ground ivy from the iris bed. No matter how ruthlessly one yanked out every trailing stem, there was always a tiny portion left just under the surface, waiting only for the encouragement of rain and sunshine to flourish again.

Breaking out of her bemused state, she ripped open the legal-sized envelope. Several bills fluttered to the floor, but she ignored them to open the single sheet of note paper.

Dear Liza,

I'm sorry to have to leave without seeing you, but perhaps it's better. I could do with a little space in which to think, and you could possibly benefit by allowing your temper to simmer down. Please refer all calls to the number I've listed below, and if a letter comes from Monterey, give me a call immediately. This should be enough to hold you until I get back, but if you run short, get in touch and I'll make other arrangements.

                                    Yours,

                                    Thatcher

Yours, he had written, the letters clearly defined and firmly inscribed. If he had any idea she'd be sitting here poring over every stroke of his pen like some moon-eyed adolescent, he might have guarded his words more carefully. Refolding the letter and tucking it into the pocket of her skirt, Liza leaned over and began gathering up the bills she had carelessly dropped. There were twelve in all, ten twenties and two fifties.

Three hundred dollars? Great Scott, how long did he plan to be gone? She could live for a month on that amount, two months if she didn't have to pay rent.

Taking out the letter again, she reread it. There was no mention at all of how long he'd be gone. She might have left the house for a day, or even two, but what if he were gone for a week or more?

With a sinking sensation, she felt the trap closing on her.

Chapter Eight

Armed with a Talbot County tourist guide, Liza went exploring. Thatcher had only been gone a single day and night, and already she felt as if she were a dried seed rattling around in a gourd. There was too little to do, with only one bed to make, one breakfast to cook, even with the dogs to look after.

She toured the indoor-outdoor maritime museum at St. Michaels Harbor, lingering a long time to admire the graceful lines of the various vessels, the pungys, skipjacks, bugeyes, and log canoes that had been built and used in the area for over three hundred years. Drawn unconsciously to another of Thatcher's haunts, she headed for the town of Easton, but halfway there she changed her mind and swerved impulsively to the right, toward Royal Oak and Bellevue. A fine fool she'd feel if the carpenters who were doing the renovation reported to him that a strange woman had been moping about the place. He'd have little trouble guessing her identity.

At Bellevue, she took the oldest continually operating non-cable ferry in the United States to cross the Tred Avon River to Oxford. The flocks of swan and mallards that paddled about near the Strand seeking handouts reminded her of Todd and the night she'd first met Thatcher. Lord, what an idiot she'd been! Talk about out of the frying pan.

Pulling her car over onto the small parking area at the foot of Morris Street, she studied her map again. Either she could retrace her steps or she could go back home through Easton, driving the long way around. And in Easton there was Thatcher's new office, not to mention the General Hospital, where he had revealed a warmth she'd seen little of since that first night.

There was no point in dredging up the best of their relationship, since she was going to have to put it all out of her mind. With a look of grim determination, she locked her car and set out on foot to explore until the next ferry returned to Bellevue.

It was long past noon when she reached the other side again, and she was starving. She didn't want to go back home, nor could she afford to treat herself

to a restaurant meal. She compromised and bought
herself a half pint of milk and a package of cheese
crackers. Then she spent the afternoon driving
through the colorful late autumn countryside between Broad Creek and Harris Creek, necks that extended inland among the fingerlike peninsulas, from
the Choptank River and the Chesapeake Bay. By the
time she reached Tilghman's Island, the end of the
journey, she was starved again. Throwing caution
and her budget to the winds, she pulled in at a restaurant that clung to the side of the road beside
Knapp's Narrows, the body of water that separated
the island from the main peninsula. During the time
it took her to order and devour her softshell crab
sandwich, she watched in disbelief as the bridge
outside the window was raised and lowered some
twenty-five to thirty times.

"Is something unusual going on here?" she marveled to the man who stood shucking oysters nearby
at a bar that extended along one wall. "Or does this
go on all the time?"

"Busiest bridge in the country," the man told her
laconically. "Don't pay to be in a hurry around these
parts, not on wheels, leastwise."

Munching the last crispy segment of backfin, she
paused to watch a minor traffic jam caused when a
sleek yawl and one of the long, narrow work boats

slowed up to allow a bugeye passage through the narrow waterway.

It was almost dark by the time she turned off on the road that led to the Hamilton house. It had been a surprisingly satisfying day. Exhausting, informative, and successful in that it had kept her from thinking of Thatcher for the most part. She turned onto the section of driveway that led to the back, where the family cars were parked, and then touched the brakes. There was a strange car in front of the house, half hidden behind the thick hedge of Russian olive that bordered the circular driveway.

Thatcher? Surely not Jeff again. Backing up slightly, she was afforded a better look at the dusty, dark sedan. Even as she watched, the driver's door opened and a long, masculine figure clad in black turtleneck sweater and matching pants emerged to stretch. The stretch disintegrated into a lazy wave in her direction, and then the waving hand dropped tiredly to rake through a thick crop of white hair.

Indecision racked her. She remembered that the Hamiltons had been the victim of thieves once, and it would be too much to have the same thing happen while she was in charge. That was her first thought. Her second was of her own safety. The nearest neighbor was half a mile away, separated by a high fence and acres of woods.

As she pulled together her scattered defenses and considered the best course of action, the tall, dark figure sauntered over to where she lingered, still safely locked in her car. He leaned down to grin through the window. "Are you a visitor, a fellow Hamilton, or some beautiful by-blow of the skeletal side of my illustrious family?" he inquired in deep, exotically polished accents.

"Who are you?" Liza blurted out. She angled the vent in order to hear better, but one hand was poised to tug it fast again if the man made any attempt to reach through the small opening.

"Richard LeRoi Hamilton, at your service, ma'am. King Richard...Richard the Dissolute, nephew to Thatcher Carstairs Hamilton and to the lovely Lady Jean. Now, if you'll lower the drawbridge, I promise not to charge across the moat until you invite me. Fair enough?"

With characteristic impulsiveness, Liza decided the man, while probably not to be trusted in the deeper sense, was harmless enough. She rolled down her window and took the hand that was promptly extended, noticing the unusually long, slender fingers and the almost womanlike softness before tucking her own fist back in her lap. "Liza Calahan," she introduced herself, "and if you're here to see your aunt and uncle, I'm afraid you've missed them." She didn't feel it necessary to offer any more information than that, at least not until she learned more about this extraordinary creature who claimed to be their nephew.

Rich Hamilton, she soon learned, was indeed a member of the clan. Over an impromptu supper of cold sweet potatoes, fried country ham, and a spinach salad, he regaled her with a few fantastic details of his life. By the time the meal was over, she had an idea that it was a largely expurgated version. Exuding an almost professional sort of charm and radiating fascinating, if decadent good looks, Richard LeRoi—or Rich the king, as he referred to himself—was a rake. Liza considered the dated term most fitting, for there was an air of almost courtly debauchery about the tall, painfully thin man. He was perhaps a young-looking forty-five or a well-used thirty-five, and the hair she had mistaken for white was instead the palest blond. His eyes, blue and faintly bloodshot, were set in pouches that did little to obliterate the sparkle of malicious good nature, and she found herself a captivated audience before the night was half done.

"My father is Uncle Car's reprehensible older brother. You see, in the Hamilton clan, as with most other ancient, royal strains, the blood is eventually polarized toward good or evil. Uncle Car, of course, is a candidate for sainthood, as is my worthy cousin Thatcher. They are possibly the only two lawyers in the history of organized religion to be canonized. Dad, on the other hand, set my sister and me a less salubrious example by repeatedly throwing the family fortune onto the tables of Las Vegas and then marrying one of those exquisite creatures whose talents consist chiefly of disrobing and striking a pose— my mother, from whom I inherited my incredible good looks, my well-developed theatrical talent, and the traditional heart of gold.''

"You're an actor?" Liza marveled, picking the kernel of fact from among the loquacious chaff. She'd left the dishes where they were, for once, and was comfortably settled on the sofa sipping Thatcher's best sherry while Rich lubricated his vocal cords from a pewter-crested pinch bottle of Scotch.

"One of the best, my lovely, although currently... resting, as the euphemism goes. To make a long story short, which, incidentally, has never appealed to me overmuch, I was invited to leave Exeter a good deal earlier than my father had planned, which left me lamentably short of academic prerequisites. Instead of Harvard, I enlisted in the Coast Guard, where I discovered a surprisingly strong aversion to following orders. The ensuing years are best left to your innocent imagination, my sweet, but after a period of, shall we say, apprenticeship in the art of living, I discovered my true calling. I have trod the boards, scintillated on celluloid, fascinated in films, and currently my distinguished features are making a fortune for the purveyors of one of the finer distilleries."

"Commercials?"

He grimaced. "I despise the word. Still, it's a living, to coin a hackneyed phrase."

Liza, now thoroughly at ease with Rich's outrageousness and feeling deliciously warm and amiable, stretched her arms above her head and yawned unabashedly.

"Critics! They smite me even in the bosom of my family! Which reminds me, lovely maiden—what are you doing here, anyway? I don't believe you mentioned it."

Liza giggled and then carefully placed her empty glass down. "I don't believe you gave me a chance," she countered. "Mine seems to be a nonspeaking part, and now, if I'm going to get a room ready for you, I'd better move before I solidify."

"I should rather imagine the opposite to be more likely," Rich observed dryly, placing his own glass on the coffee table. He stood and offered her a hand, which she gratefully accepted. It was almost twelve, and she had been up since all hours. Nor had last night offered much in the way of rest, she recalled with a sudden feeling of desolation.

"What's wrong, my dear little Liza? You haven't the features to play tragedy, you know." He switched out a light, and leaving the room in mild disarray, they crossed to the staircase together. "On second thought, perhaps you do. The long, slightly angular face, that delicately molded jawline, the expressive eyes and, ahhh, that mouth. Absurdly youthful, heartbreakingly vulnerable." He eyed her quizzically and Liza's mercurial spirits rose again. They had both imbibed rather freely, with Rich having a head start on her, she suspected, and while it only increased his tendency toward the melodramatic, her own glass and a half of sherry was making her emotions seesaw wildly.

"Tell me, my fragile dove, is my esteemed cousin responsible for those shadows in your celestial eyes? You mustn't pin your hopes there, you know. If ever I envied Thatch his disgusting strength of character—and I'm afraid I frequently did—I paid for my sin long ago." He sighed heavily and Liza almost tripped on the step.

Catching herself, she forced her feet to continue, her eyes to remain focused straight ahead, but Rich was more sensitive than she had given him credit for being. "Ahh, you didn't know about Marcie? But then why should you? Ancient history makes dull reading, especially when one sees one's own future stretching out to infinity. But I do hope your future plans didn't revolve around my cousin, little Liza Calahan."

Swallowing her misery, Liza plodded up the last few stairs. Marcie! Not only did she have to contend with Ilona Clark, who fit into Thatcher's background like a hand into a well-worn kid glove, but there was also a ghost somewhere in the background who evidently had figured strongly in the past, both Thatcher's and Rich's.

She opened the hall linen closet and lifted down a comforter, carefully averting her face as she turned to hand it to Rich. "I think this will be enough," she told him in a subdued tone. "There's a thin blanket between the sheet and the spread. I changed the linens this morning." She nodded to the room Jeff had occupied during his short stay, but Rich, instead of turning away immediately, took the blanket from her and then lifted his other hand to cup her chin.

"Calahan. Liza Calahan," he repeated softly, wonderingly. "I do believe you're my own niece, sweet child."

The scales dropped and Liza suddenly knew why Richard Hamilton seemed so familiar to her, why she had accepted him so easily, with his outrageous tales and his casual commandeering of Thatcher's whiskey and his food, not to mention a room in his father's house. "Corinne?" she whispered.

"Corinne," he echoed dryly. "My sister...your stepmother. Call Ripley, someone, I just gave birth to a full-grown niece." The hand that still supported her chin moved to caress her cheek and then dropped to its owner's side. "There are times, love, when I absolutely abhor my better nature. It crops up at the most inopportune moments—times like this, when I find myself all alone with an incredibly lovely ingenue. Perhaps it's just as well I'm inclined to be hors de combat, physically speaking, after indulging too freely my taste for quality spirits."

A glass and a half of sherry, even when one was unaccustomed, was hardly enough to produce the grogginess Liza awakened with. She sat up, clutched her head, and listened for whatever had awakened her. If it was those darned dogs again, she thought viciously, she was going to thin their ranks, starting today.

The phone jangled out in the hallway, and she groaned and lurched for the door. "H'llo," she growled into the receiver, and then, like an echo, came Rich's resonant voice over the other extension. Jeff had used it to make a call and left it in the guest room. The sound reverberated in her aching head and she tried again. "Hello."

"Liza? Is that you?" Thatcher sounded tired, not to mention extremely suspicious.

Rich's sonorous tones answered him before Liza's feeble brain could begin to function. "One of us is Liza, one of us is definitely not," he announced with droll emphasis. "How are you, my boy? How perfectly delightful of you to arrange this small surprise for me."

"Rich, what the hell are you doing there?" Thatcher barked.

"Presently, I'm fumbling around for something to cover the flesh. Liza, dear, what did you do with my things last night, or don't you remember?"

The close connection echoed in her ear, and Liza held the phone away from her head. When she started to tell Rich that he had probably left his bag downstairs, Thatcher came on again.

"Liza, get to your room and stay there! Rich, if you're still there by the time I get home, you'd better start looking for another line of work because your face won't be in any condition to support you by the time I get through with you!"

Liza was still holding the phone away from her ear, blinking stupidly into it when Rich emerged from his room wrapped in a white bedspread, looking like a leftover from a Halloween party, his pale hair standing on end. The deep pouches beneath his tired eyes were darkly shadowed. "My dear child, would it be possible for me to acquire a caffeine transfusion before the next act? Artists are unfairly vulnerable to the vibrations given off by a raging Philistine."

"Bull," Liza pronounced distinctly, turning to go downstairs. Rich's high flown rhetoric was better taken late at night with an alcoholic accompaniment. In the cold light of day, it lost a great deal of its charm. At any rate, she could do with a coffee, too, especially if, as she suspected, she was going to have to deal with *two* difficult men today.

By the time Rich appeared in the kitchen, gaunt, grayish, and displaying a distinct tremor, Liza felt slightly better. She had wrapped a slice of cold ham in bread and nibbled on it while she swallowed two cups of coffee. "Maybe it's sinus," she told him as she poured him a cup. At the arch of his unnaturally dark brow, she explained, "My headache."

"Ah, those marvelous caverns, those devilish chambers to which we owe the quality of our voice. Not the voice, itself, mind you, but the—"

"Rich, knock it off, will you? My chambers are throbbing, and having them dissected for breakfast doesn't improve matters."

"Hmm," he resonated. "An allergic reaction to the wine last night, possibly."

"I only had a glass and a half, for goodness sake! I'm not a teetotaler, you know."

"What about the Burgundy with dinner?" he reminded her.

Memory smote her. "I'd forgotten that. It tasted sour to me. Maybe it was spoiled."

He groaned. "I should have known your naïveté extended to your palate. You'd have preferred soda pop, no doubt?"

"I'd have preferred milk, if you'd bothered to ask," she informed him irritably. "Do you want me to cook you some bacon and eggs?"

"Don't be obscene. The question is, do you want me to make a discreet exit before our hero makes his grand entrance? That should be...ah—" he extended his wrist and leaned back to squint at a thin gold watch "—in just about forty-five minutes, I'd venture to guess."

"You need glasses," Liza said bluntly, feeling a powerful urge to quash the pretentiousness of the man seated across from her. His sophistication, even as jaded as it was, only served to emphasize her own gaucherie, and she needed all the self-confidence she could muster.

He scowled at her. "I have selective vision," he announced disdainfully. "And what I see before me at this moment is a scrawny, underdeveloped female who's shown abysmally poor judgment in casting the male lead for her soppy little romantic farce."

"Go to hell," Liza remarked coolly and then spoiled it by bursting into tears. She didn't bother to leave the warm comfort of the kitchen, nor did she give a single thought to the man who watched her slender shoulders shaking, his bloodshot eyes taking on an unaccustomed look of concern.

"Liza, love," he said after a while. "I won't tell you he's not worth it, because he is. We both know that one doesn't come across men of Thatcher's caliber too often in this life, but believe me, you'll be a better and stronger woman for having known and loved him, even though you're suffering for it at the moment."

"I don't want to be a better and stronger woman," she wailed, her wet face still buried in her hands.

"Yes, you do, only you're too inexperienced now to realize it. You see, Thatcher fell hard once a long time ago and discovered he had been taken in by his own youthful idealism. I've watched him through the years, not without a certain amount of guilt, if you must know—" he stroked her back soothingly as the hard sobs abated "—but that's another story. There have been women, of course, with the fair Ilona leading the pack, but Thatcher is the sort of man who's born with a vision of the ideal woman implanted in his psyche, and he must needs spend his life searching for her. Alas, when he finds the gem he's been seeking, only to discover it badly flawed—"

Liza interrupted him, lifting her tear-streaked face to say, "Rich, just cut it out, will you? I accept the fact that I don't stand a chance with him, but I can

do without this Holy Grail sob story." She could
imagine Thatcher's reaction to his cousin's going on
about his personal affairs. Like Liza, he'd probably
be torn between the desire to laugh and the need to
knock the theatrics right out of him.

She went in and dashed cold water over her face
after pulling her hair back ruthlessly first and tying
it with a string she found in her jeans pocket. When
and if Thatcher came charging in to confront the two
miscreants, there was no point in letting him think
she had taken pains with her appearance on his account. With the few breakfast things in soak, she
mixed the puppies' chow and added an extra portion for Lady, who was ravenous these days with the
drain of nursing her growing babies. They were supposed to be weaned, but they'd probably nurse as
long as Lady would allow it.

Liberally smeared with the milky mix, she backed
out of the enclosure and leaned on the fence to watch
the comical breakfast routine. Teddy was still a runt,
but he was by far the most aggressive of the litter.
And his mama obviously adored him, if her slavish
bathing and nudging was anything to go by. "Today
I'm going to break up your happy little family,
Lady," Liza announced determinedly. "Just as soon
as I've had it out with Thatcher, we're cutting our
losses and heading for Virginia. We'll leave the
Hamiltons to sort out their own problems, because

you and your son and I are apt to have a condo-in-the-making to deal with when we finally get home. We may all end up in the doghouse."

The veterinarian declared herself willing to take on the remaining pups until she could find homes for them, and Liza hung up the phone feeling as if a weight had been lifted from her shoulders. No wonder most men balked at tying themselves down with a family. The responsibility was staggering. Bad enough with pets, much less children!

Unbidden, a vision of a small boy with sun-streaked hair and warm hazel eyes arose in her mind. Before she stamped it out ruthlessly, she allowed herself a wistful gaze at the small, widely braced feet, the stubbornly irregular features. Would there ever be such a child again? If so, it would probably bear a striking resemblance to Ilona Clark, she thought miserably.

She wandered into the study in time to see Rich pouring himself a drink. He gazed at her half apologetically. "One for the road."

"Oh, Rich, I don't care. Guzzle the lot if it'll make you happy." She shrugged, automatically emptying an ashtray into the fireplace and gathering up the newspapers that lay scattered across a chair and an ottoman.

The sound of a car stopping out in front seemed to mesmerize them both. When Thatcher appeared in the doorway, haggard but looking unfairly handsome in a rumpled three-piece suit, it was Rich who broke the spell.

"Cousin, it's been a long, long time."

Thatcher eyed the tall, thin man sourly. If he was glad to see him, it didn't show. In spite of the angry words spoken earlier on the phone, Liza would have expected a warmer greeting than this. "Well, what's the matter with you?" she demanded rashly, planting her hands on her hips to glare at the man who still stood in the doorway. "Rich has come all the way from Los Angeles to see you for the first time in— didn't you say it had been six years?" she turned to the actor for support. As the uncomfortable silence grew, she saw Thatcher's gaze move around the room to take in the untidy mess she had left last night. Why on earth hadn't she come in here first thing this morning and straightened up?

"Richard, if you don't mind, I'd like to speak to Liza . . . alone."

There was nothing out of the ordinary about his request. Nevertheless, it seemed to rivet the attention of the other two people in the room. Rich's eyes moved to Liza, revealing more than a trace of sympathy, and her own gaze clung helplessly to Thatcher's face. Neither of them moved for the moment.

Then, yanking his tie awry, Thatcher strode into the room and took Liza by the elbow, forcing her through the door at the other end of the study. She glanced back frantically over her shoulder as he ushered her into the chilly, unused formal living room and sat her urgently down on a hard, satin striped Biedermeier sofa. "Now, then, would you mind telling me just what the hell is going on around here?"

Liza opened her mouth to protest his highhanded actions, but he continued without pause. "Don't you have a grain of sense in your foolish head? Didn't you learn a single thing from that first episode? God!" He turned away in disgust, and Liza could only stare at him in open-mouthed dismay. He shook his head, and she noticed distractedly that his hair looked as if it had been groomed with a pitchfork. "I should have known better than to trust you, but so help me, I thought that by getting rid of Jeff, I'd got you settled for the moment."

Mystified, Liza continued to stare at him. She managed to close her mouth, but her eyes remained wide, their bright hue clouded now with unhappiness. "Thatcher, if you'd only tell me what's going on, maybe I could help you," she ventured.

"Help me," he echoed softly, then, turning to blaze down at her, "*Help me!* You'll help me, all right. You'll help me by coming back to Baltimore with me and staying with Ilona until I have time to sort you out."

"Don't be an idiot!" she flared back at him. "I've just about had it with your King Kong act. You can run your own little kingdom any darned way you please, but you can't run me. I'm going back home where I belong, and if anyone so much as tries to hand me a ten-dollar bill again, I'll refuse it. I don't want any more reminders of the blasted Hamilton clan!"

"Don't be ridiculous. You don't even have a job. By now you probably don't even have a place to stay, and what about those miserable, flea-bitten hounds of yours?"

"Don't worry, I wouldn't leave them here if you begged me to! We'll be out of your way just as soon as I can get my things in the car and then you can fumigate the whole blasted place after we're gone."

"I should have known better than to pick up a stray from the streets, even if—" He broke off to glare at her from under thunderous brows, his mouth like a steel trap. She had turned in the doorway to catch and throw back his final insult, but something held her silent, something in the almost tortured way he was staring at her. Without voicing the retort that trembled on her lips, she spun away and ran up the stairs to slam herself into her room. She was breathing hard before she reached that doubtful sanctuary, and it was not all due to exertion.

Taking in great, gulping breaths, she threw her things carelessly into one small bag and the cardboard box Carol had mailed her only a few days earlier. Good thing she'd saved it. It went to show that her instincts still worked, at least part of the time. It was just a darned shame her instinct for self-preservation had gone haywire. She raked her toiletries from the shelf in the bathroom and yanked her shower cap off the knob on the back of the door. Ilona's yellow silk wrapper swung there mockingly and she ignored it. The pair of them could use it to wrap the trash in, for all she cared. She'd rather have her own seven-year-old flannel than all the silk robes in China if they had to pass through Hamilton hands.

Chapter Nine

By the time she came downstairs again it had started to rain, a cold, dispirited sort of drizzle that defused the fine heat of her temper and left her feeling tired and empty. Opening the front door widely, she placed her suitcase outside and reached for the box, skinning her knuckles as the storm door closed prematurely. "Drat!" she muttered, but there was no real recharging of her anger. She needed that anger, too, for impetus to propel her through the next hour or so. Once she was out of the territory, it would be different, but she knew all too well the danger of hanging around here where any minute she might see Thatcher again. All her resolution would melt away like candle wax. "What's the point in having a healthy Irish temper when it flies out the window the minute your back is turned?'' she complained to herself, staggering under the load of baggage.

The study door had been closed when she had passed it, but she had heard the sound of the phone, Thatcher's impatient bark, and Rich's pear-shaped tones chiming in with an exclamation a few minutes later. Whatever the contretemps, it ought to keep them at it for some time, certainly long enough for her to collect the dogs and get away. She opened the back door of her matronly sedan and jammed the baggage inside. The dogs could just sit on it until they got to Dr. Mackey's.

Trying to ignore the mist of rain that fell steadily, she loped across to the dog pen. ''Come on, Lady, time to go. Here, Teddy...no, I'm not playing games with you!'' She scooped up a handful of pups and dashed for the car, head down against the rain. Just before she reached it, Thatcher appeared.

''What did you plan to do about the tire?'' He was leaning up against the trunk of her car, arms crossed over his chest. He nodded to the right rear wheel. It was riding on the rim.

''Oh, damn and blast!'' One of the puppies wriggled from her grasp and took off across the lawn, and Liza struggled with an almost overpowering need to sit down and bawl. Unconsciously clutching the other puppy in her arms, she suffered his wet laving for a long moment while she considered what to do. Thatcher was certainly no help. He just stood there, one dark eyebrow lifted in weary mockery.

"You don't have to go, you know."

Her eyes blazed to life and she dropped the dog, who dashed off after his brother. "Thanks for the gracious invitation, but I wouldn't stay here a minute longer if I had to walk all the way home!"

"Which you may very well have to do. I checked your spare and it's bald. It wouldn't get you five miles, especially on wet highway. You'd better come on back inside and let me call a garage."

She fought desperately against the unworthy desire to cry uncle, to put herself in those strong, capable hands and let nature take its course, but then she remembered those hands were planning to turn her over to Ilona's tender mercies, and that was absolutely out of the question. She was no masochist. "Dr. Mackey's expecting me. If you'll get out of my way, I'll change my tire," she said primly.

He shrugged away from the side of the wetly gleaming car. "Be my guest, but don't you think you ought to wait for the rain to slack off?"

It wouldn't occur to him to offer to change the blasted thing for her! Well, she could change a tire as well as any man, rain or no rain. Rudy had taught her that the first time he had had to rescue her on the way home from work. Pity he hadn't thought to remind her of the state of her spare when he checked her car over before she left home, but he probably thought, and rightly so, that she couldn't have afforded a new tire anyway.

"What's the matter, no jack?" Thatcher inquired politely from several feet away. He had picked up one of the pups, and the other was licking the rain from his shoe.

Face set in grim lines, Liza fumbled through the accumulation of junk in the trunk of her car. She had plenty of chains, all right. If Mother Nature was dead set on teaching her a lesson, why couldn't she have produced snow instead of a flat tire?

No jack. It simply wasn't there. She stood up belligerently and turned around to capture a look of fleeting triumph on Thatcher's face. "You have a jack, don't you? Would it strain your legendary generosity too much to lend it to me?"

"You're perfectly welcome to it, but I'm afraid it wouldn't do you much good. You see, it's a rather specialized type to fit my own car, and these older American models take a different sort. Sorry. But I do have a suggestion to offer." He regarded her with suspicious blandness, ignoring the rain that glistened on his taut skin. He had shed his jacket and tie inside and now he stood there in leanly tailored iron gray trousers, a matching waistcoat, and a silky white shirt, the cuffs of which had been turned back to reveal his muscular, hair-roughened forearms.

"Well?" she challenged him. The ignominious position she found herself in stoked the fires of her temper, and she was rapidly reaching the boiling point.

"Why don't I call a garage and have them send someone out with a tire? While they're changing it for you and patching your old one, we'll take the dogs to the vet's in my car. You did say she was expecting you?"

Liza blinked away a trickle of rain, regarding him with a suspicious glance. On the surface, she could see nothing wrong with the plan. At least he wasn't trying to force her to stay on. In fact, he seemed to be unusually willing to put himself to some trouble to speed her on her way. "You don't need to do that. I can drop them off on my way out to Highway 50."

"Just trying to save you some time. You'll be in pretty much of a rush by then, you know. By the time someone from the garage comes to change your tire and then takes the old one back to patch it, it'll be late to be starting out."

She searched his bland words for hidden barbs. There was nothing at all to be learned from his closed features. Her suspicions reluctantly subsided. "If you don't mind having the dogs in your car, I'd appreciate it."

"Not at all," he replied evenly. Crossing the expanse of well-kept lawn to where his own car was pulled up in front of the house, he opened the door and dropped the two pups inside. "You get the rest of the tribe, and I'll transfer your things."

Quick suspicion reared its head again. "But there's no point in that. I'll be going home in my own car, not yours."

"Sorry. I wasn't thinking," he murmured.

Later, seated beside him as the radials sang on the wet pavement, Liza was unable to suppress a shiver. She had gotten soaked while she stood out in the rain arguing, and as if that weren't aggravating enough, Thatcher didn't even look damp. As if sensing the direction of her rancorous thoughts, he reached over and switched on the heater, allowing a welcome stream of warm air to waft over her. From the back seat came the sound of Lady bathing her babies, and Liza pushed back a twinge of guilt at what she was about to do.

"Rich told you he was Corinne's brother, I suppose," Thatcher said as they neared the small veterinary hospital.

Fixing her glance on her knotted fingers, Liza said, "Yes."

Silent minutes ticked past, and she fought against the soporific spell of the windshield wipers. Then he asked, "Have you heard from her since she remarried?"

"I haven't heard from her since we parted company years ago."

"You didn't care for her very much, did you? I guess it was natural for a child your age to be jealous, under the circumstances. Still, she did her best for you when the time came. You'd have had no one at all to turn to when you needed help if she hadn't stepped in and made all the arrangements."

Liza studied his forceful profile, trying unsuccessfully for cool objectivity. What was the point in bringing all this up, especially now? In a little while she would have severed the last connection with her former stepmother, as well as with this cousin of Corinne's she had literally run into so unexpectedly. But because he seemed to be waiting for a reply of some sort, she said, "I don't have anything particularly against Corinne." The old resentment had gradually faded and died, with no fuel to replenish it. "It suited us both, the way things worked out, and no one suffered any lasting harm. I certainly got through it with no real problems." If you don't call being totally without spending money much of the time and living on pennies a day for over a year problems. Not to mention being paranoid for fear a social worker was going to snatch her off to who knew where, or that one of the more aggressive of the older boys who showed so much interest in her would discover that she lived alone with no one for protection. Other than that, no problems. "And anyway, it's all water over the dam now. Here . . . there's the parking lot."

"I take it you're getting rid of your precious pets," he said, a harsh note entering his deep voice. "Easy come, easy go." He pulled up close to the entrance and switched off the engine. Lady struggled up from under her burden of babies to nuzzle Liza's neck.

"It's all right, girl," Liza comforted her. "You'll still have Teddy." She turned to Thatcher. "I'm leaving all but two of them. My apartment, if it's still mine, has a rule against pets, but I can't give up Lady and Teddy." She shrugged with feigned indifference. "Maybe if I have to move, I can find someplace that'll let me keep them." Just why he should be so upset, she couldn't imagine. Why should he resent it if she got rid of the whole lot?

"You haven't heard yet whether or not your place went condo?"

Restlessly, she turned to gather up as many pups as she could carry. She didn't want to think about it now. She had other worries on her mind, not the least of which was Lady's reaction to parting with her children.

As it happened, the parting was postponed. Thatcher removed the pups from her arms and or-

dered her to remain with the others while he alerted
the vet to the invasion. "I'll be back in a few minutes to help you with the rest."

He was gone almost five minutes and when he
came back, it was to tell her that the doctor had
agreed to check over the bitch and the runt, give the
pup his permanent shots and Lady the ones she
couldn't take while she was nursing. "But I can't
wait," Liza cried. "You had no right to make any
such arrangements without my say-so!"

If she hadn't sneezed just then, she might have
held out against him, but Thatcher reminded her that
she had a rough patch ahead of her and things
wouldn't be improved by her coming down with
pneumonia. "Sit tight. I'll take in the rest of the
crew, and by the time you pass this way on your way
home, they'll be ready to be picked up. One more
worry off your mind."

It was cowardly. Chalk it up to the fact that she
was cold and wet and terribly apprehensive about
going back and finding herself without a place to
stay. Oh, yes, chalk it up to anything but the real
reason. Her unknowingly wistful eyes clung to
Thatcher's coolly impassive face. Grudgingly she
agreed. "So much for time saved. Oh, all right, but
tell her I'll be back in half an hour. That tire had
better be finished by the time I get back home—I
mean to your home."

"You can count on it," he replied firmly, gathering up the remainder of the dogs.

Fifteen minutes later, she questioned him about the route he was taking. "Shouldn't we have turned off at Acorn Creek Road?"

"I need to check on something aboard the boat. I've had some work being done, and the boys might have left things open to air out the paint fumes. I'd just as soon not have to bail her out in case the rain picks up."

Liza's fingers twisted in her lap. With the heater back on, she was no longer cold, but she felt a chill of another sort begin somewhere in the deepest regions of her mind. She stared out the window, oblivious to the beauty of muted patches of wine red and golden leaves on glistening black trunks against a backdrop of silvery rain. They twisted down the narrow graveled driveway to a private marina, and she caught a glimpse of a small wooden sailboat patterned after the working oyster sloops that plied the bay. "I didn't even know you owned a boat," she said half resentfully.

"She's a recent acquisition. I thought as long as I was planning to move back to this area, I might as well go all the way. Commuting between Baltimore and Annapolis, I didn't have time for much in the way of recreation."

"You sound as if you were going into semiretirement." She opened the door and slid out before he could come around and help her.

"Dad's stroke brought home a few things to me." He frowned momentarily and then shook his head, as if to fling away the clinging drops of moisture or an unwelcome thought. "Come on, let's get out of this rain." He took her arm and guided her onto the slippery deck. She waited while he unlocked the hatch that led to the miniature cabin below. It smelled of paint and juniper, and she inhaled appreciatively, ignoring the damp coldness.

"Give me a minute to crank up a few things, and we'll get a little heat in here. The portholes were open, just as I thought." He busied himself with a set of switches and dials, and soon an engine throbbed into life.

"Don't tell me this thing has a furnace."

"Nothing so fancy, I'm afraid. It'll warm up presently, though. Meanwhile, I can make us a cup of coffee on the gas ring. Maybe I should dose yours up with some antichill medicine." He grinned over his shoulder. Something in the lazy gleam of his eye triggered further unease on her part.

"Look, just shut the windows and let's get going. I have a long way to drive today, and for all I know, I'll have to find a motel somewhere to spend the night. At the rate I'm going, I won't make it home before midnight, if then.''

"Maybe you'd do better to postpone leaving until the morning.''

"No way!'' Her biting tone hid her own growing weakness, and she edged toward the three wooden steps that led up and out on deck. The rain sounded like thunder as it beat down on the painted deck above them.

"Sit down.''

Instead, she pushed open the hatch and started up, expecting to feel the bite of his fingers on her shoulder any second. After only the briefest of hesitations, she took the last two steps in one and burst out onto the wet deck. Turning hurriedly toward the low railing that circled the sloping decks, she saw with disbelief the widening stretch of water between the *Bay Bird* and the shore. Even as she opened her mouth to screech out a protest, her feet slipped from under her and she landed on her back.

Thatcher was beside her almost instantly. She could have screamed with rage. As his hands moved over her, testing one limb after another, she caught a wicked glint in his eye. "We've got to stop meeting like this,'' he muttered. He lifted her carefully, and Liza struggled against him until she felt his foot begin to slide. "Be still, dammit,'' he growled. "I'm not exactly dressed for this outing.''

"Then, blast you, put me down and take this thing back to shore. You've had your little joke, but pardon me if I don't think it's at all funny."

"Oh, it's funny, all right. It's hilarious, only the damned joke's on me." He dumped her on one of the padded lockers that lined the small cabin and stood up, his tall, lean body almost bridging the gap between deck and overhead.

Jumping to her feet, Liza was across the cabin in two long strides, her hands slamming recklessly against the confusion of dials and switches until Thatcher caught her by the shoulder and spun her aside. "Damn you, you'll try my patience too far one of these days, and you'll suffer the penalty! Now sit down and behave yourself while I get us to a place where we can anchor and have this out."

The cabin space was beginning to warm up nicely by now, but it did nothing to diminish the coldness that froze her into a huddled lump of misery. Having landed on the cushioned locker bench, she drew her long legs up and clasped her arms around them, cradling her face on her damp and bony knees. She was distraught at the mess she seemed to have made of her escape and disgusted with herself for the small flicker of nervous excitement that raced along her spine. As if she hadn't enough to deal with, with Thatcher in this peculiar mood, she was discovering a traitor inside her own skin.

Casting her a warning glance, he disappeared topside and was back again almost before she had time to wonder what he had been doing. She refused to ask, refused to speak at all.

He came over and swung her feet aside, sprawling out beside her, and took one of her cold hands in his. "You still haven't thawed out," he observed almost indulgently.

"You're darned right, I haven't, and I'm not going to either!" Liza blazed. At his look of growing amusement, she barged ahead rashly, "So if you have any funny ideas, you may as well get them out of your head. You can play your childish games alone."

"Not my idea of fun." His hands stroked her fingers and then turned her hand to trace the lines in her palm. Catching her breath at the streak of lightning that coursed through her body unexpectedly, she jerked her hand away and tucked it under her arm. "What's the matter, Liza? You seem on edge." He was so obviously on top of the situation that it frightened her.

"Leave me alone. Just because you . . . you picked up a stray on the streets, doesn't mean you're stuck forever! You've done your bit of social work for the year. Case closed." She was shivering in spite of the snug warmth of the cozy cabin.

"This case can't be filed away all that easily, I'm sorry to say. Liza, haven't you realized by now that you're an obsession with me? You've been an uncomfortable... an *extremely* uncomfortable obsession for the past five years, one I could well have lived without."

Shock waves rolled in on her as she continued to stare into the treacherous depths of his hazel eyes. "Five years," she repeated numbly. "But that's absurd! I... we didn't even know each other five years ago. I never saw you before that night when I barged into you at the street dance." But even as she refuted his unbelievable charge, her mind was flipping over the leaves of the past, turning to a day she had long since buried in her subconscious—a rainy day, a day much like this one, when she had stood alone, surrounded by a dozen or so people she scarcely knew beside her father's raw new grave. Corinne had not even spoken on the way to the funeral and as soon as they'd arrived, she'd moved off, standing on the other side between the lawyer and another man who had arrived alone after the others. A tall, remote-looking man whose strong, attractive features had scarcely made a dent in Liza's own insular grief.

She raised disbelieving eyes to him. He had mentioned remembering her from that time, but she'd discounted it. "But I didn't even meet you then."

"No. You ran off before we could be introduced afterwards, and I had a plane to catch and couldn't go back to the house. I saw you, though. I hardly saw anything else." His voice took on a wry, bitter edge. "A tall, gawky girl in an unflattering brown coat, with several inches of dress hanging out beneath it. A pale, bony face filled with lost-looking eyes and a pale, trembling mouth. Hair like a black waterfall, slowly getting drenched in the rain. Lord knows why, but you stuck in my mind like a cockle-bur. You cropped up in my dreams more than a few times,. and I can assure you, those dreams were no place to find a child of your age. It was damned embarrassing, if you want the truth."

"And y-you remembered after all these years?" she marveled, thawing in spite of herself.

"Oh, I remembered, all right," he said dryly. "In fact, that night when you charged into me like a one-woman stampede, I thought I was hallucinating. It was only after you dashed away that I realized you were little Liza, all grown up, and I didn't need to carry my guilty secret around like an albatross anymore."

A smile trembled on Liza's mouth at the idea of Thatcher's discomposure. She bit her lower lip in an effort to hold it back. "Now that I've been exorcized, why won't you let me go?"

He lifted one arm and rubbed the back of his neck, as if to erase the tiredness from tense muscles. "For the life of me, I can't answer that. I was one step behind you that night, and when I saw you run into the side of that van, I don't mind telling you, my whole life flashed in front of my eyes. You'd been a part of me for so long, I felt the blow as if it had been me." He grinned at her crookedly, and she took a deep, steadying breath. For some reason, her heart was hammering in her throat, choking off any possibility of speech. In a voice rough with dangerous gentleness, he asked, "What made you pick up a flea-bitten stray with a belly full of problems? Especially when you were on your way to a rendezvous with your lover?"

Straining to reach his meaning, Liza shook her head. "You mean Lady. I don't know. She just looked at me and I looked at her and there it was. Karma, maybe? I was her elephant and she was my mahout in a former life?"

"Then is it too farfetched to suppose you were once my lady?" he teased ambiguously. "And now that I've found you again, I see no good reason to let you go."

Somewhere this conversation had gotten off the track, Liza thought uncomfortably. "I don't want to be someone's pet dog," she protested. Thatcher had taken her hand again, and now his fingers were tracing the blue veins that ran up her pale wrist. She made an effort to remove her hand without being obvious about it, but he only tightened his grip, pulling her slightly off balance.

"What do you want to be?" he said, his voice a shade darker than normal. "No answer? Or are you afraid to tell me?" He had shifted her so that she was leaning toward him now, and she instinctively shrank back from touching his body. "Then maybe I can answer for you," he murmured, giving her one short pull that toppled her onto him.

The bench was too narrow for two people, and he solved that by levering her so that she lay on top of him. One of his long legs stretched out across the small cabin and braced them both as Liza collapsed on top of his hard, unyielding body. She made a small sound of protest, but it was too little too late, and they both knew it. Flame raced out of control through her body, and two thin layers of damp fabric did not constitute a fire wall.

Shifting one hand to her head, he tangled his hand in her hair and brought her mouth down until it just barely touched his. His mouth remained still, as did hers. He made no effort to deepen the kiss. Liza's senses were inundated by the texture of his lips— firm, smooth, resilient, and cool to touch for the first instant, before they grew heated from contact with her own. She inhaled the scent of his skin, the spicy,

subtly erotic blend of soap and aftershave and
something that was purely personal, and a tremor
raced through her. The strain of holding her head up
was telling on her. There was not a trace of movement in the warm flesh beneath her mouth, however, and she was compelled by some fragment of
pride to hold back her own response.

As the fierce thudding of his heart made itself
known to her, a counterpoint to the pounding of her
own, she gasped involuntarily and felt the cool air
seep around their lightly touching lips, and it was as
if she inhaled the essence of him, the scent of his
flesh as well as the smell of damp wood and the exotic essence of an expensive cigar.

And then she felt his body shaking. It took several moments for it to sink in that he was laughing,
and she twisted furiously beneath the gentle coercion of his arms. Instantly they tightened around her,
bringing her mouth into grinding contact with his
own, and without warning he was devouring her lips.
His other hand moved relentlessly down her spine,
forcing every inch of her torso into mind-shattering
intimacy with his. He rounded her hips slowly, appreciatively, spreading his fingers to massage the
sensitive flesh until it was all she could do to hold out
against him.

"Give, damn you," he growled against her mouth,
and his tongue fought its way past the fragile barri-

ers she had erected. At the taste of his sweet, seeking flesh, she was lost. She moaned, half in protest, half in supplication, and then she gave herself up to the intoxicating spell of his lovemaking.

Somehow their positions became reversed on the narrow bench, and she found herself beneath his considerable weight. The velour top she wore with her jeans had ridden up, and Thatcher managed to skin it over her head. When she shivered, more in delight than in discomfort, he covered her shoulders with his hands, splaying them out over the delicate bones. His eyes burned into the paleness of her small breasts, and it was as if he were hypnotized.

"That first night," he said hoarsely, "the night I brought you home with me, my sweet Liza, you'll never know what I felt when I undressed this exquisite body of yours. You were too far gone even to know, and I should be shot for it, but when I actually held you in my arms after all those years of dreaming, I kept thinking I'd wake up soon and no one would be any the wiser." He kissed each small, rose-pointed nipple in turn, and she almost screamed at the sudden release of sensation that coursed through her body. "It was all I could do to walk out and leave you untouched that night. Lecher," he murmured hoarsely, "voyeur... you can't come up with any names I haven't called myself. Even when I appointed myself your guardian and tried to keep a suitable distance, it was no good. I kept remembering what you looked like under those wretched jeans and ill-fitting tops you wear." Pressing his face against the sensitive skin of her throat, he tasted her, tracing the course of each tendon, meeting each throbbing pulse with his tongue.

"Say something," he ordered in a voice she hardly recognized as his. "Absolve me of my guilt, for God's sake!" And then, drawing away from her to sit hunched over, staring at the soft, gray light that filtered through the small, brassbound porthole, he said, "Tell me it's crazy, considering all the years between us and all the reasons why I should have walked away from you the minute I knew who you were. Tell me only a fool would allow an impossible dream to walk into his life and take up residence in the daylight hours as if she belonged there." He laughed harshly. "Tell me something I don't already know." He turned to her then and, moved perhaps by the stark bewilderment he saw on her face, laid a gentle hand on her shoulder. Until then, it had not even occurred to her that she was naked from the waist up. Somehow it seemed irrelevant between the two of them. "Liza...little Liza." He shook his head and managed a travesty of a smile.

"Little Liza, all grown up," she reminded him with breathless daring. She was on the edge of something desperately vital, as necessary to her as the very air she breathed. She took his hand and moved it to her breast, her eyes not leaving his as she spoke her wordless need.

All her defenses were swept away by the force of his reaction. With a groan, he gathered her up so that she was half lying across his lap. "If you won't help me, how do you expect me to help us both? I'm a man of reason. Dammit, Liza...you push me too far." His mouth was on her throat, his one hand curling around her hip as the other traced the shallow indentation that ran from the valley of her breasts to her navel.

"You're the one who brought me here," she whispered in the still air of the tiny cabin. "You're the one who won't let me go back where I belong."

His face dropped to her breast, and he lowered her to the cushion. "There's only one place you belong right now, my sweet dream. In my arms, in my bed. I've wanted you too long to hold back now, and you can't tell me you don't feel the same way."

Thatcher lifted his head from her breast as he silently willed her to give him the answer he wanted, the answer his powerful need demanded for its own exoneration.

Silently she implored him to say the words that would make it right, the words that would mean forever instead of only until he had rid himself of his obsession.

They dueled without words, using swords forged of desperation. His eyes burned with a feverish mixture of guilt, accusation, and desire, while her own clouded gaze beseeched him for the reassurance she so desperately craved. She wanted him more than she had ever wanted anything in her life before, wanted to give herself to him unreservedly. But it had to be for the right reasons. She was not the same girl who had raced headlong after Todd Hardely, convinced that what she felt was love and that that would make it all come right in the end. Through necessity, her impulsive nature had been tempered by the need to look to her own welfare, for if she didn't do it, who else would? All her instincts told her that she was no longer a girl, but a woman who knew with a timeless intensity that the rest of her life hung on the answer this man would give her, the answer to a question that even now was burning its way up through the layers of her soul. She could no more hold back the words than she could stay the flooding tide.

"Then you love me, too?"

Chapter Ten

The hesitation was imperceptible, but it was there nevertheless. Liza died in that moment. She could actually feel the color drain from her normally pale cheeks. Thatcher spoke her name, but her eyes slid away and she moved to sit up. He allowed her her freedom, speaking again in a low, tortured tone.

"Liza, please..."

From somewhere she found a strength she had not known she possessed. It got her through the next few minutes, although for a long time afterwards, she couldn't recall a single word that had been spoken between them.

Somehow they were tied up at the wharf again, and Thatcher was warning her to watch her step on the treacherous deck, as if a mere broken leg mattered now. He unlocked the car and handed her inside, touching her as gingerly as he might a piece of his mother's delicate porcelain. She could have laughed aloud. Didn't he know that nothing could ever hurt her again? Wasn't he aware of the numbness that had crept over her like a shroud? Didn't it show?

They drove silently through the slanting rain. She neither knew nor cared where he was taking her. Her body swayed gracefully as he rounded a curve in the darkly gleaming highway, for she hadn't bothered with the shoulder harness, nor, for once, had Thatcher. Her feet rested easily against the carpeted floor, her hands were relaxed on her lap. An unnatural calm seemed to have settled over her, and when he commented on a squirrel that had braved the rain to recover a buried cache, she turned to smile at him. But the sweetness of the smile did not extend to her eyes. They remained bleak, strangely lifeless, like the bruised petals of a discarded violet. She seemed to be drifting. Perhaps this was really only a dream.

Thatcher muttered a stifled oath, and his knuckles whitened on the rim of the steering wheel. Liza looked at him curiously and then allowed her eyes to fall. She watched the muscles in his powerful thigh flex as he applied the brakes with unnecessary force.

Her artificial composure remained unshaken when she was flung toward the dashboard.

"Rich's car is still here," she observed slowly, dragging herself back from the strange apathy that had overtaken her. "I suppose I'd better be thinking about dinner."

He turned to her abruptly, eyes blazing. "Damn Rich! Are you all right, Liza?" He took the hands she had instinctively flung out to brace herself, folding them gently in his own. "You see what happens when an otherwise rational man allows himself to be beguiled into believing in a daydream. We have to talk, but for the moment I'm afraid I'll have to call on your help...again. We're going to have still more company. Maybe you'd better look over the pantry and see what we need before the stores all close." He opened his door and slid his legs out, moving as if he had aged ten years. Normally Liza would not have waited for him to come around and open her door, but she was no match for the peculiar inertia that threatened to overcome her. Each word, each thought was an effort, and she wondered where she was going to find the strength to get herself into the house, much less to prepare a meal.

Rich met them in the foyer. "What the hell happened to you two?" he asked wonderingly, his jaded eyes taking in every detail of their appearance. Without waiting for a reply, he turned to Thatcher.

"They caught a one o'clock flight, our time. I took down the details so you can meet them later."

"How's Dad?"

"Fine. No problem. Doctor gave him clearance to make the trip and Aunt Jean has everything under control. My old man will check here later on tonight to be sure everything works out on this end."

Neither man noticed Liza creep away to her room. She was shivering from the damp chill that had enveloped her, and all she could think of at the moment was a hot tub. Not until she was immersed up to her shoulders did it occur to her that all her clothes were out in her car. And the dogs. She had completely forgotten them. Dr. Mackey would be wondering what had happened to her.

"How can I worry about the dogs at a time like this?" she asked herself, reluctantly flipping the toggle that allowed the water to drain away. She scrubbed herself vigorously with a towel and then, with a moue of distaste, reached for the yellow silk robe. Ilona wouldn't be here to see her, and at the moment she herself was beyond caring.

Three hours later she was in the kitchen, putting the finishing touches on a veal ragout. It would be waiting without undue harm whenever the Hamiltons arrived, and she had rolls rising on a shelf over the stove, ready to be popped into the oven. Rich had brought in her things, diplomatically keeping his questions to himself. He had been the one who told her that his aunt and uncle had broken their trip in New Zealand because Carstairs had had another small stroke. They had stayed there a few days, flown on to Maui, where they rented a condominium long enough to rest up, and had then crossed to San Francisco, where they had spent several more days with Mr. Hamilton's older brother, Rich and Corinne's father. It was from there that they had called to say that they were on their way home.

Thatcher had come into the kitchen then. It was, in Liza's estimation, the most inviting room in the house on a day like today, when the cold rain outside combined with the fragrant steam inside to fog the windows, enclosing them in a safe little haven.

She needed her head examined, she told herself ruefully. Her eyes followed Thatcher's large brooding frame as he poured himself a cup of coffee. She should have run like a whitetail deer when she'd had the chance. He'd as good as told her that while he might be attracted to her—obsessed, as he called it— he didn't love her. It might be her age. Because of her relationship with his cousin, he seemed to consider her a generation removed. Whatever the reason, there was something between them she didn't quite understand, something that had to do with her past, and for the life of her, she couldn't see what it was. She knew him well enough to know that Thatcher would never begrudge the money he had spent on her when she was too young to fend for herself.

A frown touched her clear brow. And still, it seemed to revolve around that time period. Surely he didn't blame her for being a burden to his young cousin, in spite of what he had said. If there was one thing she had *not* been, it was that.

"I'll be leaving for the airport in a few minutes. Liza, I'd appreciate it if you could find time to change the linens in my room. Dad and Mother will want to be downstairs, so I'll move back up to the front room."

"Hmm," Rich muttered, stroking his long, thin nose thoughtfully. "I forgot to tell you, old man, but Lonie called. When I told her what was up, she said she'd be in sometime tonight to look after things."

Thatcher dragged an impatient hand through his already untidy hair. "To look after what, for God's sake? Mother can't stand Ilona. Why didn't you head her off?"

Rich, clad as usual all in black, shrugged his slat-thin shoulders. "To look after her own interests, to answer your first question, and as to the other, fair Ilona hasn't listened to me since I suggested she might manage to pass sixth-grade math if she spent as much time on her books as she did on her looks."

Interpreting Thatcher's harried expression, Liza spoke up with quiet determination. "Look, I'll get the beds done and have dinner all ready, and then I'll be on my way. Ilona can have my room, and as for anything else—"

"You'll do no such thing!" Thatcher barked. He grabbed a well-worn suede jacket from a coatrack and rammed a fist into the sleeve. "I'll expect to see you here when I get back. See to it, Richard." With that he was off, slamming two doors behind him in angry succession and leaving Rich and Liza to stare at each other in amazement.

A slow, knowing grin broke over Rich's sallow features, giving him the look of an elongated elf. "So that's the quarter from whence blows the wind. After all this time, I'm stunned."

Liza blew an explosive breath out between her teeth and strode across to remove a head of lettuce from the refrigerator. She ripped off the outer leaves, whammed the stem end down on the edge of the sink, and then gave a vicious twist to the loosened stalk. "I'm sick and tired of your snide little remarks, Richard Hamilton! In fact, I'm sick and tired of the whole mess." Her voice took on a deep, mocking tone. "See to it, Richard! My God, what does he expect you to do, tie me up? I'm not exactly a condemned prisoner, you know."

The cadaverous actor poured himself a glass of the wine she had used with the veal dish and sat down on one of the rush-bottomed chairs, gracefully crossing one of his long legs over the other. "Poor little Liza, you really got in over your head when you wandered into this scene, didn't you?" He shoved a salad bowl closer when she reached for it. "You're really in love with him, aren't you? Does he know that?"

She stared at him balefully as she ripped the damp lettuce leaves into bits. "If he didn't before, he does now."

"Meaning?"

"Meaning I told him," she snapped.

His eyebrows lifted skyward. "Was that wise?"

She gave a short burst of laughter. "Since when have I had any claim to wisdom?"

"Well, my dear, as I've only known you since yesterday, I'd be at a loss to say, but you strike me as being too foolishly ingenuous to handle an affair with a man like Thatcher with any degree of finesse. Nor could you be expected to." He stopped when she showed signs of imminent apoplexy.

"Maybe I'd better tell you something about my esteemed cousin, lovey. It won't make all your dreams come true, but it might explain why he tends to be just a bit more resistant than the normal male when it comes to making that final commitment." He downed the last of the dry white wine and poured another glassful. "You see, when Thatch was just out of law school, I made the mistake of bringing around one of my...ah...ladies. Marcie was a cunning little angel, all bright innocence and big blue eyes. The only thing was, she had an eye to the main chance, and she rightly tumbled to the fact that that chance was a good deal better with a budding lawyer than a third-rate actor.'' He smiled ruefully. ''You see, on occasion I can be as honest as the next fellow. Fortunately for me, my ego can handle it.''

''Well?'' Liza prompted when it appeared that Rich was lost in a reverie of appreciation for his own nobility.

''Yes. Well, Thatch fell hard. He'd been far too busy slogging the books to take up more frivolous pursuits up till then, and with his bar exams staring him in the face, the poor fool popped the question, got the answer he wanted, and was all but salted away permanently when he discovered that little Marcie had been a bit careless.''

''Careless?''

''Or shrewd, as the case may be. With girls like Marcie, you can never be sure. At any rate, when Marcie kept pushing to tie the knot without delay, in spite of the fact that Thatch was up to his noble ears in studies, I began to wonder. I mean, Marcie and I were no longer attached, but we hadn't been exactly platonic friends, you understand. At any rate, I got the truth out of her and made her tell Thatch. I figured if he still cared enough for her to marry her, then they'd have my blessing and I'd enjoy the little Hamilton sprout with a clear conscience.''

The silence was broken by a wind-driven branch scraping the side of the house. Liza felt numbed by what she'd heard, and when the numbness began to wear off, she got up from the table and stood staring out through the steamy window to the darkness beyond. She didn't need to ask what had happened. Somehow, knowing and loving Thatcher as she did, she knew the way he'd react. He was an idealist, an old-fashioned man in some respects. Perhaps if his Marcie had told him in the beginning about the baby, he might have found it in his heart to forgive her. He was an extremely generous man, as she had cause to know, but she had a feeling that in certain cases he could be icily unforgiving.

Turning away, she covered the salad bowl with a damp paper towel and replaced it in the refrigerator. She was aware of Rich's sympathetic gaze on her, not that it mattered. Nothing much mattered at this point. She almost wished she could get angry again. Maybe she had run through her ration of emotions for the season. Lord knows, she'd rocked along on an even keel all these years, except for occasional spurts of temper and a few impulsive moments, until the night she'd blundered into Thatcher. From then on, things had gone from bad to worse... or from bad to wonderful, depending on your point of view. There might be something to be said for having loved and lost, but at the moment she couldn't think what it was.

The Hamiltons arrived in a burst of excited laughter, bringing with them the scent of cold rain and Chanel No. 5. Thatcher stood slightly behind his parents, rising above his father's own considerable height and towering over his petite mother. A second before he introduced them it occurred to Liza to wonder if he had explained her presence in the household, and if so, how?

Rich embraced his Aunt Jean and shook hands with the tired-looking older man. "Good to see you both. Got fed up with all that sunshine and high living and decided to come home to a nice wet Eastern Shore autumn, huh?"

Carstairs Hamilton lifted his nose and said, "Veal. And unless my nose lies, a hint of thyme." He grinned broadly and enveloped Liza's hand in both of his own. "So you're Corinne's little girl. Funny, the way fate plays tricks on us sometimes. Thatch told us about running into you a few weeks back and persuading you to help out until he got over the hump with the new offices."

Liza couldn't help but wonder just how much else Thatcher had told them, but as everyone was tired and hungry, there was no time to find out. At least they seemed grateful for her small contribution, and she was doubly glad she had taken the extra home economics course in high school.

After dinner, Jean Hamilton insisted on helping out in the kitchen. "My dear, you don't know how much I've missed it. Car kept saying if the good Lord had wanted him to go traipsing all over the world, he'd have been born a 747 instead of a small-town lawyer, and I'm beginning to feel the same way." She was putting away the Bristol Rose dishes Liza preferred to the more formal china in the unused dining room. "I guess all you young things think nothing of strapping on a backpack and taking off for parts unknown, but Car and I just got started too late. Car was forever getting established in his practice, mainly because he didn't decide to specialize in maritime law until Thatch was almost grown. By that time I was a confirmed stay-at-home." She grinned companionably, and Liza wondered how any two women could be more different than Jean and her niece Corinne. Jean's short, curly gray hair still held traces of gold, but her face had surrendered comfortably to laugh lines, as well as a few worry lines that Liza suspected were of recent origin.

They were discussing housekeeping equipment while Liza made coffee and Jean put away the last of the dishes. "I get along all right with washers, but every vacuum cleaner I've ever met has been my sworn enemy from the start," Liza declared.

"If I'd known you were going to be here, I'd have left a letter of introduction to Maudie Hoover. We've learned to tolerate one another over the years, but she can still act up with strangers."

"Like digging her heels in whenever she comes to a rug, and trying to hide behind every piece of furniture, not to mention falling apart at the drop of a hat," Liza giggled.

"And as a last resort, she sulks and snaps up her cord!" They were still laughing over the silly personification when Thatcher pushed open the swinging door. "Are we to have coffee in the study tonight?" he teased, his eyes going from one of them to the other with an expression Liza found difficult to interpret.

"Wait for the last drop to drip through," said Jean.

"Dad's turned in, but Ilona's here, so it will still be five cups."

It seemed to Liza that there was an apologetic note in his deep voice, and she remembered what he had said about his mother's dislike of the blond decorator. So much for the old family friendship, she thought with amusement on catching an exchange of looks between mother and son. What held true for one generation didn't automatically extend to all others, it seemed.

Jean went first to hold the doors, and Thatcher carried the coffee tray into the study. Liza, following half a dozen steps behind, was in time to see the brief touching of cheeks between the two women before Ilona turned her way with a rather overdone look of surprise.

"What, you're still here? My dear child, I thought you'd be long gone by now." The gray eyes were decidedly cool again, and Liza could barely repress a shudder. It had only been a day or so, after all.

Thatcher placed the tray on the coffee table, and Ilona rose from her wing chair and moved toward the sofa. But Jean took her place on the middle sofa cushion at the same time and reached for the silver pot, her level gaze on Ilona until the younger woman resumed her place in the chintz-covered chair. Liza slipped onto the ottoman near Rich's chair, feeling almost as if she were watching players on a stage. There was Jean, of course, the character part, in her heathery blue suit skirt and cashmere sweater. There was Rich, the epitome of, if not a villain, a jaded roué, and Thatcher, the obvious hero.

Her eyes wandered to Ilona, dressed tonight in her favorite honey and charcoal combination, this time in a figured silk. The heroine, of course, with costume carefully chosen to harmonize with the setting—the warm paneled walls and the gray, gold, and russet Oushak rug.

And Liza herself? A nonstarter, a member of the audience whose gaze just happened to tangle at that moment with the hero of the cast. He took the cup from his mother's hand and brought it across to her. "Liza, yours, with cream and sugar." His voice was low, unusually intimate. She avoided his touch as she took the cup and saucer from him. He pulled the other ottoman away from in front of Ilona's chair and moved it close beside Liza. "Do you mind too much sharing the front room tonight?" he asked in the same low undertone. "I'll sleep in yours, but there's no reason to move your things. Rich will be leaving tomorrow, and we can reshuffle again."

"Oh, but..." Liza began, dismayed at the idea of sharing anything with Ilona Clark. Her uncertain glance moved from Thatcher to Rich, and she saw the gleam of malicious humor sparkling in the latter's slightly bloodshot eyes. "Sure. That will be fine," she agreed helplessly. She'd be leaving herself tomorrow, and this time she wouldn't make the mistake of announcing her plans beforehand.

"I wonder if my tire has been fixed," she murmured, and then could have kicked herself as she watched the sudden narrowing of Thatcher's eyes. The strongly molded features assumed their all too familiar grimness, and she searched for a topic of conversation to sidetrack his attention. "The new place—have you started on the apartment remodeling yet?'' she asked brightly, and then groaned inwardly as Ilona's head lifted abruptly. Oh, rats! It was probably supposed to be some sort of a secret, a surprise that she didn't expect Jean would welcome.

That, however, was no concern of hers. She'd be well advised to keep her mouth closed until she could escape, because it seemed she put her foot in it every time she opened it. There was a period of tense silence, broken only by the settling of an apple wood log in the fireplace, and then the phone rang, startling everyone in the room with its shrill demand.

''Catch it, Thatch, before it wakes Car,'' Jean demanded softly, and Thatcher leaned forward to reach the phone that had somehow found its way to the unused piano.

''Uncle Frank? Yes, we are…mmhmm, about half an hour ago.'' There was more along those lines, and Thatcher assured his uncle that the patient had arrived in good condition and would be seeing a doctor first thing in the morning. ''We'll keep you posted. Would you like to speak to Richard?''

It seemed he wouldn't, and so the conversation was terminated. Liza stood and carried her cup to the tray, collecting Rich's as well, and then said something about going up to redo the beds.

''Leave it,'' Thatcher ordered. ''I think it's time we all turned in. One way or another, it's been a hell of a day.'' He grinned and his gaze moved lightly around the room, coming to rest on Liza. His hazel eyes penetrated her fragile defenses, and she felt the color rise to her cheeks.

To cover her confusion, she gathered up the rest of the coffee things, rattling cups precariously in their saucers as she placed them on the tray. There was absolutely no reason for her embarrassment, but that didn't change the fact that she felt somehow humiliated, and when she was humiliated, she tended to react with anger. It was all very well for Thatcher to toss out commands—do this, do that, stay put. When she had foolishly held out hope that he might be coming to care for her, she'd allowed herself to be manipulated for his own obscure ends, but not anymore. He had rejected her love and as good as told her by his silence that he didn't love her. She had too much pride to hang around to wash his dishes and warm his bed. He had Jean for the one and Ilona for the other, leaving no place at all for Liza Calahan.

She was in the blue room, gathering up her night things, when he came in without bothering to knock. "Just a minute. I'm almost gone." She snatched her lacy, sheer nightgown up against her breast and pulled the navy flannel robe from its hanger, oblivious to the incongruous combination. Her gaze skimmed across the bottom of his corduroy trousers, unable to lift to his face.

"Liza, look, I'm sorry about all the confusion. I know you and Ilona don't exactly hit it off, but just for tonight, would you—"

"No problem," she declared airily. "If she can stand it, I certainly can. After all, there are two big beds in the front room."

He lifted a hand to the back of his neck in a tired gesture. The action strained the black knit of his shirt across his shoulders. "We need to talk, Liza, only I'm not sure this is exactly the time and place." His eyes touched on her hairbrush on the dresser and moved deliberately to the bed she had turned down, the pale blue sheets she'd slept on last night.

Reacting instinctively to the kindling intimacy of his glance, she swung past him toward the door, lips clamped tightly and flags of color flying in her cheeks. Never again would he trick her with his potent masculine charm! The scent of expensive tobacco and the subtle, mossy aftershave he used assailed her nostrils, driving her temper even higher as she recognized her own weakness.

"Liza." He spoke softly but sharply, reaching for her arm as she breezed past him.

"Don't you *touch* me!" she seethed.

"Liza, what the hell's got into you now?" he demanded with weary impatience.

"Nothing's got into me! I'm just sick and tired of you and your domineering ways. Just because I—"

she broke off, aghast at her own rashness. She had been about to blurt out the fact that she loved him...again. "Just because for a little while I put up with your high-handed manners—do *this. Don't* do that. Stay *here,* go *there.* Hop into my bed for a few minutes between peeling potatoes and taking out the trash!"

He caught her around the neck and almost pulled her off balance as his stunned face peered down at her. Belligerently, she glared back at him, seeing the swift display of emotion—the disbelief, the anger, and then the growing amusement.

"That's right, laugh at me. The skinny kid in the outgrown coat and the drooping skirt, with the wet hair dripping down her back. That's what you remember, isn't it?" She was in full spate now, and not even the tightening grip on her nape could slow the words that tumbled from her lips. "And then, when the same scrawny girl makes a fool of herself in front of your very eyes, you can't pass up a chance to keep her around for laughs. Is that why you won't let me go whenever I try to leave here?" She was shivering now with the very force of her own emotions. She wished she'd never started it, because she couldn't seem to stop. "Did it amuse you to see me fall apart every single time you so much as touched me? Oh, that must have been hilarious! You and Ilona probably—"

He shook her then. "Stop it. You don't have the slightest idea what you're talking about, Liza," he growled. His fingers were digging into her neck, and she'd be sporting a new set of bruises by morning. It was only fitting. She'd leave here the same way she arrived, looking like a positive hag.

"Liza, Liza, you put yourself through entirely too much agony, and I assure you, it's totally unnecessary." He drew her against him, and to her shame she found herself accommodating her body to the muscular hardness of his, as if she were a bit of lichen attaching itself to a tall, strong tree.

"At least it's a symbiotic relationship, not just parasitic," she grumbled against his neck.

"Wha-a-at?" He laughed. She could feel the vibrations deep inside his chest, and instantly her breasts reacted by tightening into sensitive peaks. She leaned away to frown up at him and witnessed the swift changes that came over his features—the widening of his pupils, the flattening of the planes of his face. A flush of color appeared in the coppery hue of his perennial suntan just before his mouth came down on hers.

Conquered without firing a shot, she thought helplessly, her arms stealing up around his neck. The gown and robe fell heedlessly to the floor as she opened to his thrusting kiss, and she was utterly unable to hold back her eager response. As one by one the nerve centers of her body caught fire, the reasoning part of her brain shut down, leaving her as vulnerable as a leaf in a hurricane before the strength of his passion.

At last he lifted his mouth, his breath coming in warm, shuddering gasps against her cheek. "God, Liza, what is there about you that drives a man to the point of distraction?" he groaned. "If there's a fool in the room, I'm it. You make me forget everything else, forget all reason, all the promises I made myself. Just stop it, will you? Turn it off!"

Still high on the intoxicating spell of his potent masculinity, she was unable to speak. She clung to him, craving more... more than he was willing to give, more than she had ever asked of a man before. With her face held tightly against his chest, her eyes lighted on the bed, and it was all she could do not to move toward it. After all these years of being the strong one, of saying no and making it stick, she wanted to be the weak one now, to succumb to his complete dominion, only it was Thatcher who held back.

He put her from him, his cheeks still flushed and his eyes feverishly dark. "It's a damn good thing I didn't actually meet you five years ago. I'd be selling shoelaces for a living on some street corner."

Hope fluctuated treacherously. "You mean, I'm bad for you?" Liza whispered.

He rested his mouth on her hair, speaking in a husky growl. "I mean I can't take much more of this. Good or bad, you're going to have to—"

The soft, scented quietness of the French blue room was invaded by the harsh summons of the phone again, and Liza jumped away from the arms that held her.

Thatcher swore softly, lurching for the instrument before it went off again, but Liza was closer. She dashed to the hall, lifted it, and spoke into the receiver, glancing over her shoulder at Thatcher, who stood in the open doorway. Farther down the hall, another door opened, and then another, and as Liza murmured the words, "Hello, this is the Hamilton residence," she was acutely aware of the curious glances from both Rich and Ilona, although the blonde's piercing gaze was rather more malignant than curious.

"Liza? Liza Calahan?" A woman's voice grated angrily in her ear. "So it really is you! I thought Rich was up to his usual tricks." There was a pause during which Liza racked her brain for a clue to the caller's identity, and then it came to her.

"Corinne?"

"It's Corinne, all right, you little troublemaker. Perhaps you'd be so kind as to tell me just what the hell you're doing there. How did you get Thatch's address?"

"But I didn't—"

"What lies have you told him about me?" the voice ran on vindictively. Liza held the phone away from her ear and looked helplessly at Thatcher. She avoided glancing at either of the other onlookers, but she could almost feel the probing fingers of their curiosity. Dismayed, she could only stand there while Corinne's almost incoherent words rushed over her.

"What's going on?" Thatcher mouthed as he finally removed the phone from her nerveless fingers. She could only shake her head. It was like waking from a warm, sound sleep to be inundated with icy water. Corinne sounded almost drunk. Surely she wouldn't be so enraged about Liza's having met the Hamiltons if she were sober. It was absurd. It made no sense at all.

Ignoring the others, Liza moved like a sleepwalker into the bedroom and stood staring at the two garments that had fallen to the floor. She picked them up, her mind half caught up in unpleasant memories, half tuned in to Thatch's occasional monosyllables.

Ilona appeared in the bedroom door. "Who is it?" she demanded in a harsh undertone. Thatcher was only a few feet down the hall.

"Corinne," Liza told her lifelessly.

"What does she want? Corinne never cared two bits for anyone but herself. I can't imagine her bothering to call at this hour of the night just to check up on Car's health.''

''It's earlier out there. If you don't mind, I'm going to bed now. You're using the bed by the window, aren't you? I'll take the other one.''

Ilona slanted her a suspicious look, but Liza was beyond caring any longer. Let them sort out their tangles among themselves. She couldn't begin to keep up with her own problems, much less anyone else's. Corinne evidently had something on her mind, but in spite of her irrational accusations, Liza couldn't imagine what it had to do with her. They had parted on good enough terms and had had absolutely no contact with each other since then. It had been five years since Fred Calahan's pitiful estate had been probated, leaving his widow with the little that remained and his daughter with just enough to keep her in peanut butter and gym suits until she graduated and could go to work.

Only she kept forgetting. It had not been her father's money that had supported her those last few years. It had been Thatcher's. Corinne had evidently felt sorry for her because there was so little left, and rather than allow her to think her own father had been negligent in not providing for his only child, had borrowed from Thatcher to make up the difference.

Too exhausted with the events of the day, she crawled in between the chilly percale sheets and closed her eyes gratefully. Who knew where she'd be sleeping tomorrow night? It wouldn't be the first time she had pulled a Scarlett O'Hara. I'll worry about that tomorrow.

Chapter Eleven

The shaft of brilliant sunlight that slanted across her pillow awakened Liza the next morning. Still groggy from the aftereffects of a heavier than usual sleep, she threw back the covers and padded barefoot across the faded pink and green lilies that adorned the soft blue carpet.

The rain had gone, taking most of the remaining leaves along with it. They were plastered on every visible surface, some floating on the quiet ripples of the river. Those that clung stubbornly to the rain-blackened trunks of the trees glowed incandescently against dark green conifers. The sky was an incredible pale turquoise, tinged with gold near the horizon, and for long moments, she stood there, drinking in the freshly washed beauty of the Maryland countryside.

And then, like tiny cloud shadows, fragments of memory began to chase across her mind. Shoulders sagging, she turned back toward the room to discover Ilona's enigmatic gaze on her, and she shivered involuntarily.

"Get back under the covers. I just heard the furnace come on. It'll be warm in a minute." The strong light was not particularly kind to the older woman, and it occurred to Liza that Ilona might be closer to Rich's age than to Thatcher's. Nor did Ilona make any effort to disguise the circles under her eyes or the fine crow's-feet that radiated out at their corners. Her lips were pale, much thinner than they looked when carefully made up, and there were more lines falling from the pinched-looking nostrils to bracket her twisted mouth.

"Go ahead," came the mocking contralto. "Look your fill and gloat over being barely out of your teens. But when you're long gone from these parts, I'll be Mrs. Thatcher Hamilton."

Liza drew the covers up around her protectively, not moving her gaze from the woman on the other bed. "I haven't heard Thatcher mention any engagement."

"Don't worry, you won't. You won't be anywhere near here when that time comes, and believe me, darling, it's coming. He's had his little fling. *Twice* he's had his little fling, and there have been a few minor episodes in between, but when it comes time to settle down for the long haul, he'll choose one of his own kind.''

Liza continued to stare at her, feeling her eyes begin to sting as she forgot to blink. She was afraid to blink for fear of squeezing out the tears that lay just under the surface. She'd do well to get her Irish up again, because if she didn't, she'd be swimming in a pool of self-pity, and if there was one emotion she detested, it was that. ''I haven't seen any signs of a grand passion between you two, unless you've done your courting in his offices. I must say, it's a bit chilly there for that sort of thing.''

"Don't worry your little head about our courtship. After Marcie and then you, Thatcher's due a relationship based on more adult values.''

Liza could almost pity Ilona Clark. With a little more effort, she might manage to pity Thatcher for being married to a bloodless clothes horse. She was half tempted to let Ilona go on thinking what she so obviously thought, but perhaps she owed Thatcher that much, at least. In years to come, she'd hate to have this cold, contemptuous creature throw up his misdemeanors whenever he wouldn't toe the line she drew. ''I hate to disillusion you, but there's nothing of that sort between Thatcher and me.''

She felt herself taken apart and put back together again by a merciless gray stare, and then Ilona said, "You know, I almost believe you. I should have known that after Marcie, Thatcher would be a bit too fastidious to get involved with another of the same sort. I suppose it was a case of trying to do his duty and being taken advantage of again." While Liza attempted to make sense of the first part of the charge, Ilona continued. "But you're excess baggage around here as of now, darling. There's nothing to keep you from walking out that front door and heading for Norfolk, or wherever you call home. If you're a bit short of funds, then I'll be glad to treat you to a tank of gas."

The two women eyed each other warily. It was Liza who broke the uncomfortable silence first. "What do you mean, another of the same sort?"

Penciled eyebrows lifted, causing creases in Ilona's pale forehead. "What do you think I mean, darling? Poor Thatcher made a complete fool of himself over that cheap little floozy Rich brought here years ago, and was actually on the verge of marrying her when he discovered she was pregnant—and it wasn't Thatcher's doing, in case you're wondering." She waited expectantly, a look of avid malice on her washed-out face. "Poor Thatch is a dinosaur in this day and age. He'd never dream of compromising an innocent young thing like Marcie."

"I know all about that," Liza said quietly, "but I don't see any resemblance between Marcie and me, unless you mean she was a lot younger than he was. He certainly doesn't want to marry me, so what are you so concerned about?" The unsteadiness of her voice in no way robbed her demeanor of its unusual dignity.

Ilona sat up then, one peach-colored satin strap falling from her shoulder. Her smile was one of purest malice. "But darling, I'm not at all concerned. You see, I know all about you and your precocious love life. You forget, Corinne and I were pretty close between her various marriages." At Liza's frown of bewilderment, her eyes narrowed on a gleam of malicious triumph. "Oh, she told me all about it. Poor Thatcher. It came so soon after the Marcie thing that he was thoroughly disgusted. He's a soft touch, though, and when Corinne came crying to him about her wild little stepdaughter getting herself in trouble with a man, he jumped on his white horse and came riding to the rescue, as Corinne knew damned well he would. Tell me, Liza, as a matter of curiosity, didn't you study elementary biology in your school? I thought they taught sex education in the third grade these days."

The voice went on and on, but Liza had ceased to hear it. In a trance, she saw the lips moving, saw the avid glint in the cold gray eyes, but it meant nothing to her. A minute later, she stumbled out of bed and raced to the bathroom, where she was violently sick.

By the time she emerged, Ilona was gone from the bedroom. She must have used another bathroom. Liza couldn't care less. Her only concern now was to get out of this horrid situation without having to see anyone, without having to pretend she didn't know what they all thought of her. There was no way she could explain that it was all a pack of lies, no way they'd believe her, a perfect stranger—or an imperfect one, she quipped silently, with slightly hysterical bitterness. Family was the sacred cow, the holy of holies, as far as the Hamilton clan was concerned. They might not even like each other very much in some instances, but if blood was thicker than water, theirs was solid concrete.

She was in the hall, headed cautiously toward her old room, when she heard the front door downstairs open and close. She flew silently to the window to look down at the garage. Thatcher and his father were climbing into the Mercedes. Jean had mentioned their running into Easton General this morning, so that meant she had only Rich, Ilona, and Jean herself to avoid.

She nearly wept at the thought of Jean Hamilton's private opinion of the girl she had found installed in her home. It must have taken all the composure at the older woman's command not to let on how she really felt. Briefly, Liza considered seeking her out and trying to explain about what had really happened all those years ago, but she gave it up with a defeated sigh. Corinne was Jean's niece. Whatever else she might be—a liar, a mercenary opportunist—she was still a Hamilton under all her three marriages.

Liza managed to collect her things within ten minutes. Rich had brought in only her suitcase the day before, not the box Carol had sent, so it was no problem getting everything jammed in the scuffed old suitcase. She tiptoed down the front stairs to the foyer. The others were in the kitchen, judging from Rich's mellifluous tones, at least. He was holding forth as if he had an audience.

Her car was sitting squarely on four inflated tires; she didn't dare risk checking on the spare, for fear there wasn't one there. She'd just have to trust to luck. First stop, Dr. Mackey's Small Animal Clinic. She should have plenty of time to be across the bridge before Thatcher got back. For that matter, why go back that way at all? It would be shorter to head south on Route 50, and the Bay Bridge Tunnel toll wouldn't cost any more than the extra mileage. The main thing was to be gone as quickly as possible, to forget this whole episode in her life had ever taken place.

Her badly bruised spirit told her that forgetfulness would be a long time in coming.

The waiting room at the small clinic was full, cats on the cat side of the reception desk, dogs on the other, and a boy with an incredibly sad-looking spider monkey perched uncomfortably on a corner of the coffee table. Liza took her place at the counter and waited for the receptionist to get around to her.

"Calahan," she told the girl when her turn came. "I left a litter of pups and their mother here yesterday."

The girl turned away to a filing cabinet and spent an extraordinary amount of time shuffling through the folders. Liza fidgeted. The door opened and closed three more times before the pert young receptionist returned to tell her that Dr. Mackey wanted to see her before releasing the dogs. Liza had no choice but to wait. She leaned against the wall and stared at the harsh green indoor-outdoor carpet and wondered again what on earth she was doing here so far from home, waiting for two dogs she couldn't support, and a doctor whose bill she probably couldn't pay—wondering about anything except how she was going to get Thatcher Hamilton out of her system.

His image kept imposing itself on the noisy, smelly little waiting room, and she could see his strong, beautiful face, the features sometimes tender, sometimes brooding, often angry, she admitted with a

wry, inward smile. Her imagination conjured up a
vision of broad, reliable shoulders clad in a worn
chamois shirt, and it was so overpowering she could
smell the familiar scent of wool and tobacco, of
mossy aftershave and some essence that was pecu-
liarly Thatcher's, an erotic essence of healthy masculine flesh.

So deep in her daydream was she that it took the
nudge of a red-faced, redheaded woman with a Ger-
man shorthair pup to alert her that her name had
been called several times.

"Miss Calahan, if you'll come this way. Dr.
Mackey wants to speak to you."

It seemed the tests were not all in yet, and as the
dog had been found wandering in a state of near
starvation, it was important that she be given a
thorough going over. "We can't rule out heartworm, you know," the woman veterinarian said, and
Liza felt herself grow cold.

"Heartworm! It sounds awful. Is it really that
bad?"

The explanation took some time, and when Liza
walked numbly out through the crowded waiting
room again, she saw nothing except for Lady's
warm, amber gaze. She held Teddy close to her. He'd
been given a clean bill of health, and the doctor had
told her that she could settle up for them both when
she picked up Lady later on that afternoon.

She drove aimlessly for some time, oblivious to the fact that she was rapidly depleting her tank of gas and getting no closer to Virginia. The puppy had given up chewing on her glove and had fallen asleep in the seat beside her by the time she found herself on a vaguely familiar road, a narrow, graveled driveway through a dense stand of pines and sweet gum. The sun shone brilliantly, and a fresh breeze that was colder than expected had sprung out of nowhere.

"This is ridiculous," she muttered, rousing from the mindless daze that seemed to have her in its grip. "I've heard of being possessed by one's possessions, but I never expected to be in that position myself." She began to look for a place to turn around. If she were smart, she'd take the puppy and head south, leaving Lady for Dr. Mackey to place as soon as she had been given a clean bill of health. She drove slowly, winding through the resinous-smelling trees that grew close on each side of the road. There was absolutely no place to turn around, and she wasn't inclined to attempt to back out to the highway. "Darn it, Teddy, you're no help," she exclaimed, half laughing. The puppy roused to stretch and then slept again. "If there's one thing I've always had plenty of, it's a lack of possessions, and now look at me. I can't even get out of this blasted county on account of a pair of soulful eyes gazing at me from behind bars." Lady had been in a small wire cage when

Liza had seen her. Her tail had thumped eagerly, then slowly drooped when she realized she was not to be released.

"Oh, damn and blast!" Liza muttered. She found herself in a small clearing on the Miles River, staring at a glistening turquoise and white sailboat, its single mast sparkling with a brand-new coat of varnish. "Blast it all to bits." She buried her face in her crossed arms on the steering wheel.

The puppy slept soundly while Liza cried until there were no more tears. It occurred to her as she sniffed and fumbled for a tissue that part of the emptiness she was feeling was perfectly justified. She had eaten little the day before, and her reaction to Ilona's shattering revelation had been physical enough to deplete her. Nor had she eaten anything since. At this rate, she'd be in no condition to cope with getting herself, much less her two charges, back home. Now that she had a family dependent on her, she'd better straighten out her act.

Taking a deep breath, she rolled down a window and allowed a current of air to blow directly in her face. It felt freezingly cold on her tear-wet cheeks; she relished the bracing sensation. She was warmly dressed in navy corduroy jeans, her lavender pullover, soft, crepe-soled boots, and coat in matching cinnamon-colored suede. She raked her fingers through the heavy silken swathe of black hair, tossing it back over her shoulders, and put on one of her gloves, deciding against trying to retrieve the other from under Teddy's jowls. Switching on the engine again, she backed around and then turned toward the driveway... and slammed on the brakes.

There was a maroon Mercedes parked squarely in the middle of the road. Even with the sun glinting on the windshield, she had no trouble recognizing Thatcher in the driver's seat. She fought against a wild flare of exhilaration. A breathless sort of inevitability settled over her as he unfolded his considerable length from under the wheel and strolled over to where she waited.

"Were you looking for anything specific or just out enjoying the spell of good weather?" he asked mildly. He braced an arm on the top of her car and leaned over so that he could watch her reaction.

Feeling like a complete fool, she could only sit there, hating his eyes on her now that she knew what he thought of her. She stared straight ahead, struggling to come up with something smart and devastating to say... and could think of nothing at all.

"Why don't we go aboard? At least on a day like today, you won't be risking life and limb on a wet deck." He opened her door and held it expectantly.

"If you'll move your car, I have other things to do. You're blocking the way." She refused to look at him, but there was no escaping the penetrating scrutiny from those golden green eyes. She could feel them raking over her, taking in every detail of her appearance, and her fingers tightened on the wheel until her knuckles were blue white. "Please!" She dragged the word out unwillingly. She *hated* to beg, hated to be in a position of having to ask anything at all of this man who thought he had every right to the contempt he felt for her. How he must have enjoyed playing with her these past few weeks! Cat and mouse, with the poor dumb mouse overwhelmed with gratitude each time the paw was lifted and it was allowed its freedom for a moment. Only the cat realized it was all just a game, knew all along that there was only one possible outcome in the end.

"Get out, Liza." The tone was soft, even gentle, but there was no mistaking the underlying note of steel.

Briefly, she considered defying him. She stared at the heavy car blocking her way and ran her eyes along the edges of the small clearing. On one side, the trees grew all the way down to the water, and on the other, a grove of tall reeds, their seed heads glowing purplish gray in the sunlight, waved before the wind. They grew in swampy terrain. She'd find herself mired in the mud if she tried to escape that way.

"Satisfied? You may as well come along, Liza, because there's only one way out, and until I decide to allow it, I won't be leaving here."

With a sigh that was almost like relief, she glanced at the puppy. The sun came through the window, making his downy, light brown coat gleam like mink.

"Leave him. He'll be fine in here."

He walked ahead of her, not even turning to see if she was following. The arrogance of his attitude enraged her further, and she stalked along over the hard-packed ochre clay, her arms wrapped defensively across her chest. Any other time she might have appreciated the mellow beauty of the autumn landscape, with silvery bare tree trunks framing the deep blue of the bay. There were half a dozen snowy sails in view, and across the mouth of the river, the sun glistened on a pale field of cornstalks left standing for the benefit of wildfowl hunters, dried tassels waving in the brilliant sunshine.

Thatcher turned to assist her over the low wooden rail. Her gaze swept the freshly painted deck. "What, no plank to walk?"

He grinned, and she averted her face from the subtly triumphant gleam she saw in his eyes. "I'm on the other side of the law, remember? Although there was a time, I suspect, when the two sides weren't all that far removed."

He opened the hatch and she preceded him down, inhaling again the pungent mixture of juniper, teak, and fresh paint. Light reflecting from the river outside danced across the overhead, and she stared at it hypnotically as she waited for what was to come next. A feeling of resignation had all but robbed her of her will to resist.

"Would you like a cup of coffee?" Thatcher inquired. He was doing something in the small space that constituted the galley, and Liza was suddenly overwhelmingly aware of her stomach.

"I don't suppose you have anything to eat on board, do you?" she asked in spite of herself.

"I'm afraid not, unless..." He rummaged through a small hanging compartment and took out a tin. "Unless you'd care for a few dry crackers. Probably stale by now."

She took the tin from him and pried off the top, delighted to find a poor commercial imitation of Maryland's famous beaten biscuits.

The water was soon boiling on the tiny gas ring, and Thatcher made instant coffee for them both, adding sugar and powdered cream to hers. She had seated herself crosslegged on one of the cushioned lockers, the same one, she thought with burning awareness, on which he had made love to her the day before. Just before he handed her her mug, she began to uncoil herself, in case he thought she was inviting more of the same, but he urged her back.

"Stay put. I'll sit over here." His eyes crinkled then, narrowing on a glint of humor. "It's the only way we'll ever get any talking done."

"I don't think we have anything important to talk about," Liza muttered through a mouthful of dry biscuit.

"Don't you? I wouldn't have taken you for a quitter, Liza Calahan."

Her eyes fell to the chipped mug of steaming coffee. "I don't know what you're talking about. I haven't quit anything."

"Liza," he prompted softly, but she kept her head stubbornly down, refusing to be drawn under his all too potent spell again. She should have known it was a misguided tactic on her part. The only way to win with a man like Thatcher Hamilton was to face him down, not to try to avoid the issue.

He was beside her before she was even aware of his movement. With ominous deliberation, he removed the mug from her unresisting fingers, the opened tin from her lap, and placed them on the handkerchief-sized chart table nearly. "I know of one surefire way to get your attention, you stubborn little Irishman."

Her head flung up, her eyes flashing. "I'm not an Irishman! I'm an American woman of Irish descent."

"Semantics, semantics. They won't gain you any time, you foolish child." His hands were on her shoulders now, working their way under the supple leather of her coat. She leaned away from him against the sloping wooden bulkhead. "Liza, look at me. *Look* at me, damn you!" He clamped her chin with his thumb and forefinger, forcing her face up, but she kept her eyes stubbornly averted. His voice was deceptively soft, but there was an unholy gleam in his eye that she could see as clearly as if she were staring right back at him. "No comeback? No snappy answer? All right, since you're in such an unusually docile mood..." He let the veiled threat hang there. Catching her off guard, he pushed her sideways, and before she could sit up again, he followed her down, forcing the air from her lungs with his considerable weight. His sheepskin coat and her suede one fell open and the heat of their two bodies flared instantly.

Her mouth opened to rage against him, but he caught her angry words and ground them back against her lips. At first she struggled to slide out from under him, but as it became all too evident that her struggles were only exciting him, she grew still. And then his kiss changed, grew seductively gentle, and she was lost again. Under the firm sweetness of his mouth, she felt her response flicker and grow until she was stunningly aware of every fiber and sinew of his strong body. Her hands, trapped beneath his chest, curled restlessly. He shifted slightly so that she could slide them around his waist. His own hands left her face, where they had held her captive until she became a prisoner of her own needs, and moved slowly, in exploring fashion down her throat, seeking out the hollows of her collarbone before sliding to her small, pointed breasts. As the sensitive nerves there sent frantic messages racing through her body, she grew still.

Her eyes closed, lips parted moistly, she traced the slow, deliberate course of his searching hands down the hollow slope of her waist and over the infinitesimal swell of her abdomen, and then she felt him shudder.

"Oh, Lord, it's hopeless. How am I supposed to deal with you? We have to talk and as soon as I get close to you, I go haywire." He broke off with an exasperated oath and sat up, lifting her to sit beside him. She felt as helpless and bereft as a day-old bird flung out of the nest. "Liza, how could I have known? You've got to believe me. It wouldn't have mattered, even had it been true. Not now...not now," he repeated softly.

All the bitterness at Corinne's unconscionable action arose in her, to mingle disastrously with her own turbulent emotions. "How can you be so certain it isn't true? I mean, after all, it's only my word against hers." Her eyes, dark with passion, cloudy with pain, accused him. "And she's a Hamilton," she pronounced with biting finality.

He shook her gently, turning her somehow in the process so that she was facing him again. "Liza, I don't blame you for being bitter. It was a terrible thing to do, and only a weak and desperate woman would have considered it. That's no excuse, Liza, but try and understand. Don't let your anger poison your life."

Shifting her eyes from his compelling gaze, she fought against the gentle coercion of his logic. She didn't *want* to be made to understand, to forgive. She had been viciously slandered, and she hurt. She hurt abominably, and she wanted to lash out at the injustice of it all. "I don't care," she muttered. "I just want to be left alone."

"To lick your wounds in private," he taunted. "I wouldn't have considered self-pity to be your style, Liza. You strike me more as a type to land on your feet and bounce back fighting when you've been knocked flat."

"What do you know about it? You never got knocked off your pins in your silver-plated life."

"Sterling, Liza, please," he insisted, a tremor of laughter running under his deep voice. "And for your information, I'm still in the process of trying to pick myself up after a real knockout."

She slanted a disparaging look at him. Marcie? Surely he couldn't still be suffering for his misplaced idealism all those years ago. The thought shafted through her like a steel blade. "What knockout?" she demanded disbelievingly.

Turning away from her for a moment, Thatcher adjusted a small heater and then turned back to slip her jacket from her shoulders. It hadn't taken long to dispel the damp chill from the small cabin; she was beginning to feel overheated already. She allowed him to toss her coat on the other bench, and then he slipped his own sheepskin coat off, as well. "You're getting red in the face, and I wasn't sure if it was temper or temperature," he teased.

"I am not!"

"Liza, Liza. What a volatile package you are. I'm going to have my work cut out for me in years to come; I've already resigned myself to that."

If she had been pale before, she could certainly feel the fire in her cheeks now! She was breathless at the implication of his words. "Thatcher, I don't know what you're getting at, but—"

He laid a finger over her mouth. "No, I don't suppose you do. One thing at a time, though. Allow me to organize my case before presenting it."

Her tenuous grip on composure hopelessly lost by now, Liza knocked his hand away and glowered at him. "To hell with your case! I'm not letting you get me all mixed up again, Thatcher. I can't think straight when you start playing your hateful little games with me, so if you have something to say, then say it.''

"All right, you wild-eyed termagant, I will." His voice cut through the slightly stuffy atmosphere like a sword through butter, but there was an unmistakable twist of laughter in his wide, firm mouth. "I love you, Liza Calahan, and I'm going to marry you as fast as the law allows, and maybe even faster. So stuff that in your pipe and puff on it!"

They were facing each other like boxers in the ring, and Liza stared at him in shocked fascination. Her arms crept slowly up her shoulders and she hugged herself tightly. "Ooh," she whispered. "Honestly?"

"Yes, honestly." The laughter was all but out in the open by now. "Or dishonestly, if you prefer. All I know is that I'm not letting you out of my sight until I've got you attached to me with every legal device in the book."

Unconsciously shimmying herself closer to him, she reached for the collar of his soft gray flannel shirt. "Say it again," she breathed wonderingly, searching his face for reinforcement of his words.

"Which? That I'm not letting you out of—"

She shook her head violently. "No. The other, the . . . the love thing."

His deep laughter rang through the cozy cabin, reverberating from the heavy wooden timbers, and Liza felt an insane inclination to laugh, too. He gathered her in his arms and she fell against him willingly, entwining her arms around his neck in a stranglehold. "Tell me," she insisted.

"That I love you? Lord, woman-child, I've been telling you that in a hundred different ways ever since that night when you almost knocked me down in town." His mouth touched her eyebrow, first one, then the other, and dropped to her nose to trace its short, straight length. She twisted her head so that he brushed her lips, and then they were lost in discovering the countless ways to express love with a kiss.

"I knew I should have stayed on the other bench," he whispered hoarsely some time later on. They were lying side by side, barely able to cling to the narrow cushioned surface. "Before we go any farther, I want to set the record straight, Liza love."

"How far?"

"What do you mean, how far?" He leaned back to regard her suspiciously.

"I mean how far can we go after you set the record straight?"

His mouth was a stern line, but his eyes glittered suspiciously. "You wanton hussy! I suppose you expect me to seduce you here and now."

"I has me hopes," she allowed modestly.

"You has your nerve," he came back, his mouth quivering with amusement.

"Let's hurry up and get all the unimportant business out of the way," she urged him, insinuating her hands inside his shirt to feel the rapidly increasing thunder of his heart. "I think you need something to calm you down."

With a deep, shuddering breath, he drew her hands out of his shirt, holding them clasped in one of his. His other hand played over her hair, brushing it away from her high forehead as he gazed intently into her eyes. "Liza, listen to me, darling. Old business first, and then we'll both get on with the new. Five years ago, give or take a few months, I saw a girl who stuck in my mind and my heart in spite of every logical, rational argument I could come up with. A few weeks later, I got a call from Corinne. She was distraught. It seemed her stepdaughter had landed herself in trouble, and it was going to take a large sum of money to get her straightened out—money Corinne didn't have. What was she to do? Where was she to turn? I asked a lot of questions. Not even for a cousin was I about to hand over the sum she asked for without knowing exactly how it was to be used. I was told that it would cover hospitalization, either immediate or several months later, depending on what the doctors advised."

Liza winced, marveling even now at the staggering deception. Thatcher saw and pressed her face into his throat. She felt the vibrations of his voice with her lips as he continued to speak.

"Not once did she come right out and say that you were pregnant, but it was the obvious implication, what I was meant to think. I was sick at the idea, physically ill. You were my dream child, my beautiful secret fantasy. I had enshrined you so securely, and now you were wrenched away. It all but killed me. I sent the money, and then I went out and got drunk for the first time since my undergraduate days."

A sigh shuddered through his large body, and Liza wrapped her arms around him, longing irrationally to take his hurt onto herself. "How did you find out it wasn't true?" she whispered.

"I heard enough last night to make me wonder, and Rich got the rest out of her. She was drunk—drinking, at least—and in over her head again. Corinne inherited her father's weakness for gambling, I'm afraid, and she was in hock to some pretty heavy characters five years ago. Most of what your father left had been transferred to her name. That much I knew already. And it was child's play for her to manipulate the rest so that you got only a fraction of what was coming to you. And the criminal thing," he said, as if the words themselves were agony to speak, "was that she left you alone to fend for yourself at an age when a girl is particularly vulnerable. For that alone I could almost kill her."

Slowly, from the security of Thatcher's arms, Liza murmured, "Now I see why it was so important for me not to raise any questions. Corinne said it was to keep the social workers from dragging me off and putting me in some kind of a home."

He exploded. "If I ever see that woman again—"

"Hush, hush," she soothed, stroking the lean hollow of his cheek as it sloped from the chisel-shaped bone. "Look, I was incredibly stupid. It was my own fault for not coming out of the fog long enough to find out what was going on." She drew away from him and frowned slightly as something occurred to her. "Thatcher, are you sure I won't bore you? I'm not particularly bright, but if you'd let me study architecture, I—"

"Later, after I've had you to myself for a while, you can study anything you want to. It's time the Hamiltons branched out into another profession. But, Liza love, don't ever underestimate yourself. You're a strong woman, a beautiful child-woman who is what she's made of herself, and I've lived with you in my mind and heart for five years now. Allow me to know what I want. And in case you ever wonder, I'd have loved you even if all Corinne told me had been true—a dozen times over. I've always loved you. I always will. It's as simple as that.''

"Well...I have my good points, I'll admit, but I'm not very sophisticated. Not like Ilona," she warned him.

"No, thank the Lord." He grinned. "I'm afraid a little bit of Lonie goes a long way."

"Nor Marcie?" she ventured hesitantly.

"I see Rich regaled you with my earlier indiscretions. My cousins—both of them, I guess—have a tendency to overdramatize. Marcie was a shrewd little girl who knew what she wanted and had the looks to help her get it. Fortunately, I came to my senses in time, thanks to a little straight talking from Rich. I believe Marcie wound up marrying an undiscriminating yacht broker, and Rich's son now has a half sister."

Liza searched her mind for any other dangling threads. Finding none, she said, "Now...if that's all the old business, darling, could we please get on with the new?"

* * * * *